A GOBLIN POSTMAN CHILLER

THE

HANGMAN'S

GARDEN

PATRICIA BOW

This book was first published in 1999 by Cora Verlag GmbH under the title *Der Garten des Henkers*, in German translation. *The Hangman's Garden* is the original (and revised) English text.

Goblin Postman icon created by Patricia Bow

Cover image: "Abandoned Cellblock/Eastern State" by P.W. Baker (http://www.flickr.com/photos/pwbaker/980714864/), used by permission of the image creator and in accordance with his Creative Commons license.

Contents

Prologue

THE MOMENT SHE SET FOOT on the bridge, he knew it. He stood at the oval window that was called the Hangman's Eye, and he watched her come.

The Hangman's Eye: the men had given it that name. They'd spread the story, how the old bastard could see all over the island by that window. Likely, though, the Hangman himself had started the story. Nothing like a reputation for seeing and knowing all to scare the men into line! Not that it had done the old bastard much good, in the end.

He left the window and moved to the garden. She had chosen her path and this was where she would come, this garden.

How he hated it! The blue flowers more than all, how he loathed them! He'd have burned them out long ago if he'd been able, he'd have reduced the whole stinking place to ashes.

But fire had never been his to command. Water and darkness, yes, and sharp-edged steel, but never fire. He slashed at the flowers, although that gave him no real satisfaction.

Never mind, none of that mattered now. She was coming, with her death-shadowed mind, her sweet life-filled body. She was coming to set him free. Then he would have his satisfaction, and everybody would know it.

Soon. Any moment. He paced, and slashed at the flowers, and held a face in his mind. And now also a name. Nora.

Chapter 1

Lost

NORA'S FIRST GLIMPSE of the bridge to Holdfast Island would have been her last, if wishes had been magic carpets and able to fly her straight home.

To be accurate: it was not her first glimpse, it was her second, that did the damage. At first look, the bridge was a beautiful structure that melded well with the surrounding land and water. Its beams, of some close-grained wood that had weathered to a silvery grey, were massive yet graceful, their lines clean. At the near end, tall posts on either side held up a carved wooden sign that arched across the space above the bridge. Climbing scarlet roses swarmed up the posts and partway along the arch, so that all Nora could read on the sign was HE LOFTUS SCHO.

She turned from her study of the bridge. The driver had the taxi's hood up.

"Can you get it going again?"

"Yeah." He stood with arms crossed, watching the engine, which was steaming like a volcano. Nora wondered if he was going to do something about it, or just watch.

"Um, when?"

He narrowed his eyes at her through clouds of steam. "Fifteen, maybe twenty minutes yet till she's cool. Then we'll see."

"Twenty minutes!" Nora looked across the bridge again.

That was the second glimpse.

The sunshine went away just like that. Rain bounced off wet

2

black steel. The bridge was just wide enough for a single car or truck to pass. Steel gates closed off both ends. A narrow hut stood to one side. A man in a uniform stepped out of the hut and looked at her.

Nora blinked. Rain, steel, hut, man, all gone. She remembered to breathe. Lifted her face to the sun. Cautiously looked at the bridge again. All as before: silvery wood, rose-draped arch. *O-kay....*

Okay, but she'd hoped all that crud was over and done with. Maybe it was, she thought hopefully. Maybe this was just a one-time thing brought on by stress, and by being tired. The trip from Ottawa by way of Toronto had taken fourteen hours by train and bus and she hadn't slept much on either bus or train.

And of course being overheated and dehydrated would make things worse. Maybe it was as simple as that. Waves of heat shimmered off the black asphalt. Sweat trickled down her neck and added to the swampy stickiness of her T-shirt. Who knew it could get so hot way up here in the north woods? She pushed damp hair off her cheeks and wished she'd had the sense to buy a couple of bottles of water when she'd had the chance, back in that little village. She also wished she'd had the foresight to wear shorts instead of jeans.

The driver was still watching his steaming engine. "Um, hey." She gave him a wave. "Did you say twenty minutes? That long?"

"Long?" He shrugged minimally, saving effort. "You could wait. Or you could walk."

Holdfast Island was a shimmer of cool green on the other side of the bridge, across the sparkling waters of the channel. That is, it looked cool, compared to this stretch of potholed blacktop. Beyond both ends of the island, Georgian Bay stretched to the horizon, a soft turquoise line between the sparkling deep blue of water and the pure azure of sky. *Water, water everywhere.*

"Is it far? To the school, I mean."

"Depends." He didn't say on what.

3

All at once, Nora didn't care how far it was to the Loftus School. Anything would be better than standing here, where there wasn't even any place to sit, and broiling her brain. "Okay, I'll walk."

"Cross the bridge, turn right, quarter mile." He leaned against the hot metal of the car's roof and tilted his baseball cap over his eyes.

Nora scrabbled in the back seat and pulled out her smallest backpack, the one with her change purse in it. "What do I owe you?"

"'S paid for."

"Oh, good. And you'll bring my other stuff?"

"Yeah, yeah." He tilted the hat some more. He looked as if he might be taking a nap right there. Nora wondered if she should tip him. She hadn't had much dealings with taxi drivers, not on her own like this.

"Um..." She unzipped her change purse, picked out a toonie, since it was the largest coin, and held it out between thumb and forefinger. The driver stared at it a moment, then plucked it delicately. "Many, *many* thanks." It sounded like sarcasm. Maybe a toonie wasn't enough?

"So, g'bye!" She slung the strap of her bag over her shoulder and started across the bridge. Each step of her sandals rang it like a wooden xylophone.

She stopped in the middle to lean on the railing and gaze down at the white-crested water. Her stomach tightened. The channel between island and mainland was narrow here, and the water churned through as if driven by a turbine. You'd never swim that. Fall in there and you might never surface again. The current would snatch you away and that would be the end of you.

She pushed away from the rail and walked on, brisk but calm. *Calm.* Her stomach slowly unclenched.

At the far end of the bridge two more tall posts stood up. Here there was no sign, but a wire stretched between the posts ten feet up in the air. Climbing roses draped posts and wire, weaving a shaggy red-green arch. Past that the road started up again, not asphalt now but dirt crusted with gravel. It forked left and right. Left followed the shore; right ran into the woods.

Right, the taxi man said. Nora chose the right fork. A few steps, and the cool green shade of a pine forest closed around her. She stopped to unstick her T-shirt from her ribs, pulled in lungfuls of resin-scented air, and walked on. Quarter mile? Five minutes at most, right? If she walked fast. Maybe ten if she dawdled and looked at things.

Fifteen minutes later, the road narrowed to a plain dirt track. There was no sign of the school. Nothing but dark pines and cedars and thick maples, with here and there the chalky white of a birch spiking the dimness. A harsh cry tore the silence and Nora flinched. Then laughed at herself when a blue jay flashed across the path.

"Let me guess," she said aloud. "My taxi driver doesn't know his right from his left." She looked around and listened. No roof, no chimney, no fence, and not the faintest sound of a human voice. She might have walked into Neverland. How could the island be this big? Better start back.

Turning, she took a step, then halted. A corner of stone, unmistakably something built, showed through the pines. She wilted with relief. *Okay: forget the darn path, I'll cut straight through the woods.* She stepped off the path and pushed between thickly interlaced pine boughs. The boughs pushed back. After a struggle during which she nearly left her backpack in a bush, she stumbled out into a clear space alongside a high stone wall.

The wall was broken by a tall, round-topped gate. It was closed. Nora stood rubbing her scratched arms and wondering if this was the back door and maybe she should go around to the front. The gate didn't look as if it was used much. The planks were weathered a

5

scabby grey, and the iron handle was red with rust.

Well, no use just standing there. It wouldn't open itself, would it? She pulled at the handle, then pushed, and finally got both hands on it and pulled upward and leaned back with all her weight. The gate screeched open so suddenly she fell over into a nest of pine needles.

She scrambled up, scooped up her backpack, and stepped inside. The gate banged shut behind her as if blown to by a gust of wind. She stood looking around. Her heart sank. What kind of a place was this? It didn't look anything like the pictures on the school's website.

You'd think the woods had come into the schoolyard with her. Scrub maples and wild grape vines wrestled each other for supremacy almost up to the gate. They formed a screen she could hardly see through. The actual grounds must be on the other side of.... Wait.

Somebody was there, on the other side of the screen of brush. A sketch of black against sunlit green, flickering back and forth through gaps in the leaves. He was pacing restlessly, thwacking at the long grass with a stick. Like he'd been waiting there a long time and was getting bored. Waiting for her, maybe.

"Hello! I'm here!"

No answer, but the thwacking sound stopped. The warm air hung still.

"It's me, Nora! Nora Brook!"

Still no answer. He was ticked at having to wait, she could get that. Okay, but she was plenty ticked herself by now. "Hey! Is anybody there? Anybody? Because I'm hot and it's been a long day and..." She listened. Nothing. "Oh, all right!"

She pushed into the screen of brush, backpack up in front to protect her face. A twist and yank and she fought free into the open and dropped her pack on the ground.

She stared. Closed her eyes. Opened them. No, this wasn't a moment of weirdness like on the bridge, this was real. She turned in a

6

slow circle. The restless person with the stick wasn't there. Nobody was there. But for the moment she forgot him, whoever he was. Forgot all about being tired and hot and fed up.

This was not the Loftus School, not possibly. It was someplace completely other, unexpected. An amazing place to find by pure accident, by choosing the wrong fork in a forest path. A secret, magical place. A walled garden hidden in the heart of a dark wood.

Chapter 2
Secret Garden

INSIDE THE STONE WALLS, under and out from under the trees, waist-high tasselled grass tangled with giant ferns, black-eyed Susans, daisies, fireweed, buttercups, and a dozen other green and blooming things Nora couldn't name. The lush growth breathed sweet moisture into the warm air.

And everywhere, climbing among the ferns and saplings, were wiry vines with fine, feathery green leaves and tiny blue flowers. A beautiful, clear blue they were, deep blue as a young child's eyes. The vines ran rampant over the walls, so thickly that in places their blueness hid the grey stones.

It looked like a picture out of a fairy tale. An enchanted garden, impossible and disturbing. Nora forced a laugh. "The only thing missing is the enchanted prince!" Unless the guy with the stick had been him. If so, the prince had no manners at all and she didn't care if she never got to meet him.

She knelt down to touch one of the tiny blue flowers, six pointed petals joined at a centre of radiating darker blue. She sniffed it, then sat back on her heels. It smelled strange, pungent, like medicine. She rubbed her nose and sneezed. Shouldn't have touched it, maybe. Might be something toxic, like poison ivy.

Her shoulders moved uneasily. There was something not comfortable about this secret, scented, sunlit place. The stone walls were a good ten feet high. "Who in his right mind builds a ten-foot wall around a garden?" Nora asked herself aloud. "There'd never be

8

enough sun, except at noon."

She stood up and turned in a circle. Towering pines crowded around the outside like a second wall on three sides. On the fourth side rose a stark stone building, tall and blank as a cliff, except where the blue-flowered vines were trying to overgrow it. No windows showed except for a few tiny ones that squinted from under the roof.

"That sure as heck better not be the school, or I'm going home!"

She turned again, slowly. Someone was staring at the back of her head. She could feel it, she'd swear to it. She'd been feeling it for a while now, that creepy sense of not being alone. She stood still, gazing up at the building, then grabbed a look over her shoulder. Nothing there, nobody.

Only, just for a moment, a glimpse of thousands of eyes watching from the shadows at the base of the wall. When she looked again, it was only the sky-blue flowers, with their thousands of starry blue blooms.

"Flowers! You're losing it, girl!"

But suddenly she was sure. It wasn't just the flowers and it wasn't her over-stimulated imagination. And it wasn't from being hot and tired, either.

Someone was in the garden with her. Someone was watching her.

"Guess it's about time I stop dawdling and get to the school," she said aloud, for the ears of whoever might be listening. "They'll be coming to meet me," she added, loud and clear. Clumsy and stiff because nervous, trying not to hurry, she turned her back on the building and crunched through the waist-high meadow. Careful not to look behind, she forced a way back through the screen of scrub maples, to the gate in the wall.

When she reached the wall, there was no gate.

"I've got my directions mixed up. I just have to walk all the way around. Can't miss it that way, can I?" This time the confident monologue was for herself. Nora hitched her backpack higher and pushed on through the shrubs and vines, staying almost within arm's reach of the wall, following it with her eyes. She found a corner and kept on. No door appeared.

It did occur to her to yell for help. But what good would that do? Aside from the hidden watcher, there couldn't be another human being within miles: if there were, she would have seen or heard them. More important, she didn't want to let on to the watcher — or to herself — that she was scared. Start yelling, and that bubble of panic deep inside might pop, and then....

A scraping noise came from the other side of the wall, three feet away. Nora whirled and backed away. A hand appeared on top of the wall, clinging to the stones, then a tanned and scratched arm, then the top of a tousled brown head, then another arm, and finally a face. It goggled its eyes at her and then flashed a wide grin.

"Well, there you are!" He pulled the rest of himself onto the wall, got to his feet on top of it and stood beaming down at her, a brown-haired, gangly-legged boy in khaki shorts and a rainbow-printed T-shirt.

"So you're the one who was watching me!"

"Watching you? For about two seconds. I only just got here. Nora Brook, I presume?"

She opened her mouth to ask how he knew her name, then got it. "They're looking for me already?"

"What d'you mean, already? It's been an hour at least!"

"But I only got here, what, twenty minutes ago!" It felt like barely fifteen minutes, but she had an uneasy sense of time lost and unaccounted for.

"An hour," the boy repeated, "since your cab driver turned up at the school with your bags and stuff. He said he'd had a breakdown just across the bridge, and you'd gone ahead."

His eyebrows rose in question. His brows were steep arches over alert brown eyes, giving his whole face a ready-for-mischief look.

"He told me, cross the bridge and go right." Nora was suddenly at ease. "You'd think it would be impossible to get lost on an island this small, wouldn't you?"

The boy grinned down at her. "He should've said left. The school's about a quarter mile past the bridge, on the south shore. When you didn't show up, the Loftuses sent everybody out to comb the island."

"What made you come here?"

"I... well, I wasn't actually looking for you, to be honest. I was just grabbing a chance to explore." He looked apologetic, shrugged broadly with both arms, and nearly lost his balance. It took a lot of teetering back and forth and whirling of arms and whooping before he'd righted himself, and by then Nora was laughing. Which she suspected was just what he had in mind.

"I can guess why you're spending your summer here, doing remedial math and science," she said. "Class clown, right?"

He turned pink under his tan and put on a sternly serious face. "Come on, let's get you out." He sat down, dangling his legs. "Can you grab hold of my foot?"

She gazed up at him, baffled. "Just help me find the door, and I'll walk out."

"Door? There's no door. Not one you could use, anyway."

Nora took a deep breath. The air seemed to be thickening. The sun was pounding down like nails. "Of course there's a door!"

"Nope. Not unless you mean the one that leads into the building there." He pointed with his chin. "It's nailed shut. I know, I've tried it. The only way into the yard is the way I came, by climbing a tree."

Nora looked where he'd pointed. She saw it now, a rusty-looking slab in the wall leading to the almost-windowless building. It was nearly hidden under blue-flowered creepers. It looked nothing like the gate she'd come in by. "I guess you haven't been all the way around. My door is a gate made of wood, and it's in the garden wall."

"Nope. No gate."

"But then how did I get in?"

"Climbed a tree, like I did. Then fell in and couldn't climb out again. Hurt your head? Is that why you don't remember?"

"I didn't fall in." Her voice flattened. "I walked through a gate."

"Nora, I've been all around this place more than once. There's no, repeat, no, gate in this wall. Which makes sense, when you think about it."

"Nothing here makes sense." She pushed sweat-sodden bangs off her forehead.

"'Course it does. I mean, this was a prison yard." He kicked his sandalled heels cheerfully against the wall.

"Prison?" She looked around at the lush grass, the flowers, the trees. "This is a garden!"

"Prison. That building there, that's the jail."

"Jail? Way out here?" She couldn't stop stupidly repeating things.

"Yep. They closed it down fifty years ago. It's been empty ever since. Hey, you okay? You look peaky."

"I'm fine. Help me out of here. Please." She didn't need to ask any more questions. Everything now made grim sense. The ten-foot stone walls, the building with no windows except tiny ones near the roof. Even the isolation.

And that glimpse of a steel bridge with gates at both ends, and a man with a gun. That made sense now, too.

"It's an interesting place, really," the boy went on, as he lay flat on the top of the wall and reached down a hand. "Let's have your bag first. Okay. Now, grab my wrist. Try a jump. That's it! Up you come!

There's a history to it. Oof! It's one of the last places in Ontario where — anyone — was hanged."

Braced against the wall, gripping his wrist, her toes digging at the rough stones, Nora felt tightness grip her throat. For a moment she swung free in the air, choking, and then the air sparkled in front of her eyes, and she was falling.

SHE LAY IN a grassy meadow bathed in sunlight. A bitter scent stung her nostrils. Too sleepy to stir, having no reason to move, she lay gazing up at the soft, pure, cloudless blue sky.

Something fluttered down and brushed her cheek. She could just see the edge of it: a tiny pointed oval of heavenly blue. A petal from one of those blue-eyed flowers. Another petal drifted down, then another, until the air was thick with them. You'd think the sky had broken up into pieces and was falling down, Nora thought drowsily.

Already she lay under a cool blue blanket. Petals kissed her face like snowflakes, they tickled her chin. She tried to raise a hand to brush them away, but her hand was heavier than stone. Now the falling flowers made a sky-blue blizzard. She closed her eyes and they pattered on her eyelids. They were a weight on her body now. She opened her mouth to call for help, and choked on a mouthful of petals.

She was drowning in a flood of flowers.

Chapter 3

Heart of Water

JACK DROPPED from the wall, frightened that she'd hurt herself. She lay sprawled in a matted mass of blue-flowered creepers, gasping for breath. Her face was small and white in a tangle of dark hair. When he knelt beside her, her eyes flew open and she stared up at him. Her eyes were hazel-green, big and clear under dark brows like wings.

She caught her breath. "What— what happened?"

"Hey, that's my line." He ventured to touch her forehead with his fingertips. It was cool and trickling with sweat. "What made you faint like that? You sick?"

"No, I... Too much sun, I guess. I never thought it would be so hot, up here on Georgian Bay."

"Well, it is July. How come you're so white? You look like you've been living in a cellar all your life."

"Gee, thanks." She sat up, looked down at herself, and flicked stray blossoms from her T-shirt. Then lurched to her feet and kicked vines away from her feet as if escaping from a nest of toads. "I need to get out of here!" She faced the wall and measured it with her eyes.

"You'll need a little bit of help getting over that," he said mildly.

Nora turned and looked him up and down. "You? Okay. You'd make a good ladder." A smile lit her eyes. There now, things were getting better. "And who're you?"

"Jack McKie, at your exclusive service." He swept an extravagant bow with an invisible plumed hat. That moved the smile from her eyes to her mouth. Better and better!

When she laughed, that first time, it was like sunshine after rain. He made up his mind he'd make her laugh again, often. This summer was finally looking up!

NORA WAS GLAD to find out that she wouldn't have to walk all the way back to the bridge before taking the fork that led to the school. After retrieving her backpack they headed back toward the channel, then Jack stopped about halfway along the path, where a narrow track branched away though the woods to the south. She hadn't noticed it on her way, being so busy looking for the school.

It would have been easy to overlook even if she'd been alert for it. A deer track, Jack called it, with a casual air that meant he really wasn't sure, but thought "deer track" sounded good. For five minutes they walked south in single file, Jack in the lead, under the wind-stirred green canopy. The track meandered, then made a wide curve to follow the bank of a rivulet that came bubbling down from a rocky knoll on their right.

"A stream — on this island?" Nora stopped and stared at it. "Where would it come from?"

"Under the ground. A spring. There's a pool up there." Jack waved at the knoll. Its tree-crowned summit stood three yards above where they stood.

"Really?" She knelt on the stony bank of the rivulet and dipped a hand in. Then gasped and shook drops from her hand. "It's freezing!"

"Yeah, but it tastes fantastic! I'll bet it comes from miles down."

Nora scooped water in her palm and slurped it. She spluttered at the cold, then licked her lips. She'd never tasted water like that: stony, earthy, grassy, clean.

They walked on. Five minutes more brought them out onto the brow of a rocky hill that sloped toward the grounds of the Loftus

School. In the steep places, old railway ties had been wedged into the hillside to make a rough stairway.

As Nora followed Jack down the stairs, she took in what lay below. A garden planted in squares, a volleyball court inside a net enclosure, and a small greenhouse, all on this side of a big, solid, red brick house. It looked as if a couple of new wings had been added to the original building. Tall, spreading trees, maples or oaks, stood around the house and shaded the roof.

On the far side, where you'd expect groomed lawns if this were the city, a meadow of knee-high grass and flowers sloped to a sandy beach. A jetty ran out into the clear blue water. A small boat bobbed at the end of the jetty, and farther out in the bay a big, square wooden platform rose and fell gently. People moved about here and there among the gardens and buildings.

"Hey!" Jack jumped and waved both arms. "Hey! I've got her!"

Two of the people were suddenly hurrying in this direction, waving back. Nora squared her shoulders and put on a smile. "Hoo boy. What a way to arrive!"

"That's the Loftuses, Dr. Beth and Dr. Cuthbert." Jack led the way down the hill. "No sweat, you'll like them."

Beth Loftus was a slim, smiling woman, her grey-brown hair braided and pinned behind her head. Cuthbert was a big, shaggy-haired, untidy-looking man who beamed at Nora through thick glasses. As soon as they found out she was all right ("I just took the wrong path — I didn't mean to cause all this fuss!") they laughed and waved her on toward the house.

"Jack will take you to find your roommate," Beth said cheerfully. "Dinner's at six. Tomorrow you'll hit the books!"

Jack led the way along the near side of the house to the front. He stepped back to flourish a hand at the door, which was richly panelled and topped with an arch of glass. The rounded porch roof perched on white-painted columns and a semi-circular flight of shallow steps led down to the gravelled road that led, Nora guessed now, to the bridge.

"Okay, good," she said patiently. "This is better than that jail building, I can see that."

"And within, behold!" He pulled open the door and bowed her in.

She stepped inside and gazed. "Wow. It's like a mansion!"

"It is a mansion. It was the house where the governor of the prison lived, with his family."

"Governor?"

"That's what they called him, in the old days. Means he ran the place."

The lobby was cool and airy under a high ceiling, with white walls and a polished black-and-white checkerboard floor. A chandelier sparkled overhead. A white-railed staircase curved up gracefully in one corner.

And to think she'd assumed that brutal jail and decrepit gate had anything to do with the school!

That gate. She could still smell the sun-heated wooden planks and feel the roughness of the iron handle. It seemed so real! And yet it hadn't been there at all, had it? And who was the person with the stick? And the blue-eyed flowers, had she really seen them?

She'd drowned again, drowned in flowers this time instead of water.

"Nora?" A hand touched her arm. "You sure you're okay?"

"I'm fine. A bit tired, that's all."

Those things were waking dreams, hallucinations, the kind of things sick people see. Nora smiled at Jack, because he was nice, if a bit silly, and he deserved a smile.

And because she wasn't sick. She was just fine. There would be no more visions.

"AND THIS IS SKYE," Jack announced as a tall girl stepped down the stairs to meet them, the hem of her long, gauzy, flower-printed skirt gathered gracefully in one glittery-nailed hand. "Skye Welland."

"Skye with an 'e,'" Skye murmured, and tossed back a cloud of silver-blond hair. A mist of spicy-smelling scent enveloped her and everyone around her. It took Nora a moment to identify it as sandalwood.

Jack chortled. "Want to bet her real name is Susan?"

Skye smiled serenely and poked him aside with a thin, sharp elbow. Taking Nora's arm, she started up the stairs again.

"Welland like the canal," Jack said, climbing two steps below. "Brook like, well, a brook. Do I sense a theme?"

Skye kept smiling. "You can ignore him. He's mostly harmless."

"Like Earth in *The Hitchhiker's Guide to the Galaxy*."

"Exactly!"

That surprised Nora. Based on appearance, she'd pegged her new roommate as the kind of girl who only reads style magazines.

"We're all hitchhikers in this galaxy," Jack intoned.

Nora stopped. "Wait, I should find my bags."

"They're already in our room," Skye said. "You'll like it here, Nora. Being surrounded by water is so spiritual."

They reached the second floor, a wide corridor carpeted in soft blue, with an arched ceiling like a train carriage and three white-painted doors on each side. Light shone through a glass-panelled door at the end.

"That leads to the new wing, with the classrooms and labs." Skye pointed. "Bathrooms are at that end too, and here's our room." She ushered Nora in and shut the door smartly in Jack's face.

Nora looked around approvingly. Like the lobby and corridor, the room was bright and airy. She dropped her small backpack on one of the quilt-covered beds, the one that already held her other two bags, then crossed to the window and looked out. The view was north-west, toward the spine of the island. The forest covered the ridge, thick as an animal's pelt. The whole island might have been an animal, she thought: a bear, maybe.

There was no sign or sight of the ruined prison from here. Good.

Skye settled into a cross-legged yoga position on the other bed and arranged her skirt gracefully over her bare feet. She had the kind of pale blue eyes that went with the fair hair, and the kind of long face and long, thin nose that went with the height. She looked like a young Afghan hound, Nora thought.

"Jack's really quite bright," Skye said. "If he spent as much time studying as he does thinking up ways to be funny, he'd be a year ahead by now."

"Are there many other students?" Nora turned from the window to her bed and unzipped her bags, a big backpack and a bigger gym bag.

"No, there's just twelve of us. You, me and Jack," she ticked them off on her fingers, "all about the same age, I'm guessing — sixteen, right?"

"Right for me, anyway."

"Me too. Then my brother Bruce," Skye ticked off another finger, "a year older than me, he's here because our parents are hell-bent on him finishing school, and all he cares about is football. Then there's two younger kids, fourteenish. And six starting their final year. The older ones are no fun. They're here to upgrade their marks so they can get into a good university, and would you believe it, they're already hard at it!"

Nora hung two cotton dresses (one yellow eyelet, one plaid seersucker) in her narrow closet and crammed stacks of T-shirts, light sweaters, jeans, shorts, socks, and underwear into the white-painted dresser next to her bed. On the closet floor went a second pair of

19

sturdy leather sandals and two pairs of plain white sneakers. "And what about you, Skye? Why are you here?"

"Oh, I've been studying other things." Skye sat straight-backed, eyes closed, palms upturned on her knees. "They don't teach everything in school, you know."

"What other things?"

"Well, since you ask, things like this." Skye slid off her bed and drifted across to her dresser, where she took a small blue-enameled box from a drawer. She lifted out a silver chain hung with a shard of glittering rock and held it up so Nora could see. "This is rose quartz."

"Pretty!"

"More than that, it's a scrying stone."

"Um, scrying?"

"That's like diagnosis. It finds out things. I could use it to scan your aura, if you like. You look rather washed out."

Nora hesitated, then sat down on her bed, feet firmly on the floor. "Be my guest." She wasn't eager to have her aura or any other part of her scanned, but if she and Skye were to get along for the next six weeks, she'd better give a little.

Skye swung the pendant slowly back and forth above Nora's head. "Humm... Yes, you've been sick, that's plain as day. Let's see..." She hummed some more, then stopped the pendant. "Meningitis. Yes?"

"Sorry, not even close." Nora carefully did not laugh. "Appendicitis, then pneumonia, then bronchitis. I'm fine now, but my school year was shot. I never did get caught up on math and science." She relaxed. For a moment she'd thought Skye might really be psychic. Might be able to see really private, personal things.

After Nora washed up and changed into clean jeans and T-shirt, they went downstairs. As she stepped out the front door she nearly ran into a woman who was striding past with a heavy-looking sack on

20

one shoulder. A middle-aged woman in drab green shirt and pants, with muscular arms and short grey hair like a steel helmet. She raked Nora with her eyes, then strode on around the corner of the house.

"That's Hedda Shade," Skye whispered, when they were out of earshot. "She takes care of the gardens and the greenhouse. Jack says she's related to the people who used to live here."

Nora shivered. Such bitter eyes!

Chapter 4

A History of Death

"THAT'S RIGHT, Hedda Shade was the daughter of the last governor of the prison. Erwin Garvey, that was his name." Jack took careful sideways aim and skipped a flat stone twice over the water's quiet surface. Damn! He got worse each time, instead of better.

Dinner was over, and they had two hours of free time. The four of them, Jack and Nora and Skye and Bruce, had collected together almost without comment and wandered off to explore the island. They'd followed the sandy south shore to its westmost point, then picked their way along the rougher north side, where the hill sharpened and steepened and became a cliff. They stopped at a spot on the shore where going any farther would have meant climbing.

"Look where we are!" Jack pointed straight up the cliff. You could see the sunset-reddened prison wall, or sections of it, through gaps in the pines at the top. Nora frowned up at it and switched her gaze to the view of Georgian Bay. The sun burned a path in the water all the way from the horizon to the ripples at their toes. Red-gold light blushed on Nora's pale face and glistened in her hair.

Jack knew he was staring. Better cool it. He squinted under his hand across the bay. "Doesn't it look just like an ocean? Do you realize that the nearest land to the west is Manitoulin Island, and that's behind the actual curve of the Earth?"

"So?" Bruce casually flipped his stone at the water and watched it skip five times. He was tall like his sister, but twice as wide, and his straw-blond hair was buzzed short. He wore a permanently sullen

22

expression. Jack wondered why Bruce, who was his roommate (*lucky me!*), had come along, since he didn't seem to getting any joy out of the company or the conversation.

"So that's a heck of a lot of water, eh?"

"So?"

Jack tried not to let himself be annoyed. "I mean, think of all the ships that must've sunk out there. Who knows how deep it might be?" He deepened his voice to enhance the effect. "Deep, deep, fathoms deep."

"We could always Google it," Nora said in an edgy voice. "I bet somebody knows. It's probably all been depth-mapped, if that's the right term."

"About Hedda," Skye put in from her perch on a rock on the hillside. She had changed from her gauzy dress to faded jeans and leaf-printed T-shirt. "How do you know she's related to the Garveys?"

"I found out from one of the older kids who was here last summer. Hedda lived in the governor's house — the house where we're staying now — till she was ten. Can you imagine coming back after fifty years to your childhood home, and finding a bunch of other people living there, and the only way you can stay is by working as the hired help?"

"I can imagine, easily. She's not a bit happy. I'd love a close look at her aura. But not too close."

"If it were me, I wouldn't have come back." Nora stood at the water's edge, poised, oddly defiant. She reached out a sneaker toe to touch the wind-driven waves that frothed on the stones.

Jack found another nice flat stone, aimed, and threw. It sank at once. "Me neither, especially since her father blew his brains out in that house."

Nora looked at him, eyes wide. "Yikes! Not... not where we...."

23

"You mean what room, exactly? Dunno."

"Who cares?" Bruce flicked another stone.

"I do!" Skye said. "I knew there was a bad vibe to this place! I felt it the moment we crossed the bridge!"

"No, you didn't." Bruce aim, flicked, watch the stone skip six times. "You said it was *spiritual*."

Nora said, "How do you know all this?"

Now that he had her attention, Jack abandoned the stone-skipping competition, which he'd already lost, and settled onto a handy boulder. "I made a point of finding out about this place before I came. There was an investigation when the jail was closed, fifty years ago. Seems some bad things happened there, and Garvey let them happen."

"Bad things?" Nora blinked at the half-drowned sun. Then she shook her head. "No, don't tell me."

"Believe me, you wouldn't want to know. Anyway, Garvey was in hot water. Probably he'd have been prosecuted. I guess that's why he killed himself."

"Or maybe," Skye put in, "maybe he had no choice. I mean, it's obvious the island is just saturated with bad karma." Bruce hooted. Skye jumped up from her boulder. "It's true! He wasn't the only one to die here."

"Well, there were executions," Jack began.

"I don't mean the prisoners! I mean kids like us. Don't tell me you haven't heard that story!" Skye tossed her cloud of hair. "Guess you don't know everything, Jack McKie."

"What d'you mean — kids like us?" Nora asked. "What happened?"

"It was years ago, before we were born." Skye relaxed daintily back onto her rock. "Twenty years. Not long after the school started. Three students died." She looked around at their faces and widened

24

her eyes. "All three on the *same day!*"

"How could that happen?" Jack was annoyed at himself for having missed this juicy bite of the island's history.

"I guess it was a love triangle. Two boys and a girl. One of the boys drowned himself — just walked into Georgian Bay and swam toward the horizon. They never found his body."

They all stared out across the expanse of water. Nora shuddered. "Why would a person do a thing like that?"

"But if they never found his body," Jack said, "how do they know he drowned? Maybe he just ran away."

"They found his shoes and clothes on the beach. In fact, it was this beach right here where we're standing." Skye stabbed a forefinger down at her feet. Nora took a quick step back to the shelter of the cliff.

"Triple suicide?" Bruce put in. "Or triple murder? Like, three with one stone?" He grinned.

"It's not funny, bonehead." Skye looked at him coldly.

"No," Nora said. "Not funny. Kids dying..."

"Anyway, I got all that from Zoe, who works in the kitchen, and she got it from Mrs. Duggan, the cook, who's been here like forever. She, I mean Zoe, didn't have time to tell me more. Dr. Beth turned up just then. Seems the Loftuses don't like it talked about, and I guess you can see why."

The bright arc of the sun dipped below the horizon, leaving an orange glow behind. The air felt cooler. For a moment nobody said anything.

"So," Skye added in a matter-of-fact tone, "there's obviously a curse on the island. Probably has been for hundreds of years. Maybe thousands. Like, from the native people. By the way, we should get back while we can still see to walk."

Jack looked up the cliff. "Why don't we cut straight across, in-

25

stead of going around by the shore? It'll take half the time."

"Good idea," Bruce said, and started climbing. Skye opened her mouth to protest, then shrugged, and followed. Jack came next, then Nora. Halfway up, Jack turned and held out a hand to help Nora up a steep place treacherous with loose stones. She gave him an exasperated look and bounded past him like a mountain goat.

"I guess my mother raised me all wrong," he said sadly, and heard her laugh.

At the top they stopped and stood in a row, panting (all except for Bruce, who had to be in pretty good shape, Jack conceded) and watched the sun go down a second time. The stone wall of the prison loomed behind them, a tall golden slab in the sunset. It looked almost pleasant, sort of soft and rich, Jack thought, with that warm light all over it.

"Look, the jail's right there." He pointed. "Why don't we explore it?" A shadow of dread crossed Nora's face. He saw it and wished he hadn't said anything. Too late to take it back, though.

Skye shook her head. "At this hour?"

"Why not?" Bruce said. "Anybody scared?"

That clinched it, of course. "The sky's still light," Jack said cheerfully. "That'll give us another twenty minutes. Besides, I've got this cool device right here."

He pulled it from his pocket and showed it around, a folding knife that was like a whole hardware store in itself, including a mini-flashlight. He'd bought it especially for coming to Holdfast Island, because out in the wilderness you never knew when you might need a fish scaler or a compass or a chisel, right? Bruce picked it up, unfolded various implements, and grunted approvingly.

"This is crazy!" Skye said. "Nora, let's leave them to it."

"C'mon, Nora!" Jack grabbed his cool device back from Bruce and brandished it like a magic wand. "Live on the edge!"

She hesitated, then the shadow of dread vanished behind a stubborn look. "Why not? It's only stones and mortar, right?"

They walked around the building to the front, Bruce going first to break a path through the shrubs and vines. The front door was hidden behind rough planks, which were half-hidden under festoons of the blue-flowered creepers. It was the only outside entrance. There were no windows at this level.

"This has got to be off limits! We can't go in, obviously." Skye sounded relieved.

"Nobody's told me that yet." Jack yanked at the boards and Bruce helped him, and they broke off easily, with a squeal of rusty nails. The door, uncovered, was made of rusted metal, or metal-sheathed wood. It hung askew, loosely attached to the jamb by one twisted hinge.

The gaping doorway exhaled a stream of cool, damp air that smelled of mildewed plaster and rotting wood and corroding metal. Darkness lay beyond the slanted opening. In the forest, the birds felt the sunset and fell silent. The breeze died. The only sound was their own breathing, and that was too loud.

All at once Jack was flat certain he didn't want to explore the ruin. Not right at this moment. Another time, maybe. Then he looked at Nora, all huge, dark eyes in a too-pale face. She sent him a pathetic attempt at a smile and he tossed back a careless grin. No way he could back out now, not without making himself look like a total loser.

He detached the flashlight from his pocket knife and snapped it on. A thin beam of light shot into the gap of the doorway. The darkness inside sucked it up. "Onward!" he proclaimed, pushed aside the vines, and ducked past the broken door.

Chapter 5

Heart of Darkness

NORA WATCHED the other three duck under the creepers: first Jack, then Bruce shouldering through, then Skye, still hissing protests. The darkness swallowed them. She clenched her trembling hands.

Only stones and mortar. Right. *If Skye has the nerve to go in there, so have I.*

Lifting aside a mass of creepers, she couldn't avoid crushing some of the tiny blue flowers. Their pungent scent made her eyes water. She rubbed at her eyes and smelled the scent on her hands. It swept through her brain like a cool wind, blowing away the day's confusion and fatigue. The worst of her fear blew away with it.

She took a deep breath and edged past the slanted door. Just inside, she bumped into Skye. The two boys were a pace ahead, the outlines of their cheekbones and noses glowing like carnival masks in the darkness as Jack shone his flashlight from side to side.

"Uh... I thought it would be lighter, with the sun hardly down," he said.

"No windows," Bruce reminded him. "Stupid thing to forget."

Jack muttered something.

They stood in a low, square room with rusty steel doors on three sides, including the one they came in by. The wand of light conjured details into existence. A broken light bulb hanging from the ceiling, their own tracks in the thick dust, a wooden desk draped in a soft grey veil that Nora realized was layer on layer of spider webs. She

28

rubbed her goosebumped arms.

"Why..." she whispered. She cleared her throat and tried to speak normally. "Why's it so cold in here?"

"Because of the stone walls, I'd guess," Jack said. "They must be two feet thick!"

"It's like being inside a cave." That was it exactly. You couldn't see much, so you had to rely on sound and smell, and the feel of the air as it moved around you. A muttering echo followed their footsteps, as if the jail was a great big drum. An image came into Nora's mind of a vast honeycomb of spaces, hundreds of rooms and corridors stretched overhead and hollowing the earth beneath.

Jack's light ran across a pale square on the wall beside the door to the left, then ran back to it. It was a faded cardboard notice. AUTHORIZED PERSONNEL ONLY. He pushed the door. It squeaked but didn't move. He pushed again, harder, and it grated open. He waved the light. "Hey! I'll bet this is where the cells were."

They filed through the doorway, Nora last, and he was right. They found a long corridor with rows of metal bars on each side, all painted a muddy yellow. Broken plaster crunched under their sneakers. Without warning a big chunk fell from the ceiling and shattered at Jack's feet. He jumped back with a yelp, then laughed with not quite enough breath.

"What a horrible place," Nora muttered.

"It's just that it's in such bad shape, that's all," Jack said, stubbornly cheerful.

"No. I think it must have always been a horrible place." Ugly, with a deliberate, soul-killing ugliness.

"Well, come on! Here's another door. Let's see where it goes!" A door at the end of the corridor opened on a staircase that led up and down. Tightness gripped Nora's chest.

"The cellar!" Jack flashed his light down the stairs. "Wonder what we'll find down there?" He started down. "Watch out, the steps are cracked. There's another door at the bottom." They eased down, foot by foot, feeling each step. There was a steel handrail bolted to the wall, but Nora couldn't bring herself to touch it. Neither could Skye, it seemed.

They reached another landing and another door. The stairs crept on down into the dark. Jack poked the light downward. "D'you want to—"

"No!" said Nora and Skye together.

"Oh, okay." Jack feigned disappointment, not very convincingly. "We'll just explore this level." Rusty hinges screeched. They filed through into the corridor beyond. The smell of damp earth and stone rose around them.

"This must be where they kept the tough customers," Jack said. He swept the light up and down, back and forth. Bruce whistled. At least three of them crowded together as if for protection.

It was a gallery, Nora thought: like a huge shopping mall, built on three or four levels around a high, deep, long gulf of empty air. That was where the resemblance stopped. Here were cells instead of shops, darkness instead of brilliance, dirt instead of shine. And the emptiness beyond the rusting steel railing seemed to pull at her.

"This is amazing!" Jack leaned on the railing to look down at the lower levels. Metal squealed and swayed. Bruce grabbed him by the arm and yanked him back.

"Idiot!" Skye said.

"But look at this place!" Jack ran the light upward. The beam dwindled to a tiny dot that ran and leaped over lumpy arches high overhead and was lost in masses of swaying things

Nora thought she caught a glimpse of green up there. Moss, probably, she thought. Not leaves. There couldn't be anything in here that loved the sun.

"We've been here long enough, okay?" Skye said. She sounded snappish. Nora would not allow herself to say anything. One word and she might start to lose it.

"Just a quick look around." Jack started forward. Then came Bruce, then Skye, then Nora at the rear.

Tough customers: maybe, she thought. There was no keeping up appearances here, no plaster or paint. The walls were bare fieldstone, furred with dust. Jack brushed a finger down the wall, sending swirls of dust through the flashlight beam. They all coughed.

As the thin beam moved along the corridor, it ran across solid steel doors set in the stone walls. Each door had a tiny barred window at eye level.

"It's like a dungeon in the dark ages," Skye whispered.

Soon, Nora promised herself. We'll be out of here soon.

Something grated behind the cell door to her right.

Nora's hand froze onto Skye's wrist. "What was that?"

"Ow! What? I didn't hear anything."

"What is it?" Jack came back, shining his light into Nora's face. She shielded her eyes.

"I heard something. Like a footstep. In... in there." She pointed at the cell door.

"In there? Can't be." Jack shone his light in. "Nah."

Bruce pulled at the door handle, then pushed. It didn't budge. "This is rusted solid. Can't be anybody in there."

"All right. Mistake," Nora said grimly. "Let's get going." The light swung away and she blinked, blind in blackness. She took a step.

When a hand came up to the window in the next cell door, and fingers curled around the bars, she told herself it was an after-image from Jack's flashlight.

But as she walked the shapes kept coming, hands drifting to the

31

barred windows like moths to the light.

Nora walked on, step after step, eyes front, trying not to see the things that moved at the edges of her vision. Nothing was there. Nothing could be there. Nothing at all.

"Look, this is the end," Jack said, six paces ahead. He sounded disappointed and relieved. "Not much here after all, is there?"

"What did you think there'd be?" Skye sniffed, so elaborately contemptuous that Nora knew she was badly shaken. "Chains? Rattling bones?"

Nora cleared her dry throat. "Jack, give me that light, will you? I'd like to have a good look at something for once."

"Well, okay. But there's nothing to see. Kind of a bust, eh?"

Nora shone Jack's flashlight into the barred window nearest her. She moved the beam methodically over every visible inch of the tiny room inside. A bare cot, a torn mattress, stone walls, stone floor. Nothing more. She ignored the little voice at the back of her mind that mentioned the near corners next to the door, beyond the reach of the light, where someone could stand unseen. She walked on and scanned the next room. Dust and stone and scraps of misery. Nothing else.

There, you see?

She began to breathe normally, realizing that she hadn't drawn a full breath since the moment she stepped inside the prison. *No wonder I've been seeing things!* She laughed quietly, then made up her mind.

"All right, everybody, I've had enough. I'm going! And I'm taking the flashlight with me." She headed toward the stairs as she spoke. Pulling open the door, she set one foot on the landing and paused to let the others catch up, if they wanted to. And of course they wanted to. Here they came, Skye foremost, scurrying.

Skye was still two strides away when Nora ran the flashlight beam up the stairs. It flickered across something pale hanging in mid-air, something that moved. A hand. A hand that didn't vanish in the light.

The light wobbled up the dark column of a body and stopped on a face.

He stood looking down at her from just below the ground floor landing, a tall boy with a shock of dark hair that streamed back from his face in a wind she couldn't feel. He moved his lips soundlessly. She caught the shape of words. *Nora,* he said. *At last.*

The flashlight slipped from her numb fingers, flipped in a bright arc and smashed on the stone floor. Blackness closed on her like a giant's fist.

Chapter 6

Dark Angel

"ALL RIGHT, nobody panic!" Jack's voice was loud in Nora's ear, much too loud for someone who was so annoyingly cheerful and totally calm. His hand curled around hers and gripped, and she gripped back, hard, before making herself let go.

"Dropped the flashlight?" Bruce said. "Dumb!"

Nora found her voice and was glad it wasn't trembling. "Dumb, nothing! Somebody was on the stairs. He startled me."

"My lord!" Skye stood right next to Nora, her sandalwood scent strong even in this miasma. "Now how are we going to get out of here? I can't see my hand in front of my face!"

Jack was scuffing his feet along the floor. Metal clinked on stone. "Ha! Wait... Got it! Now, if we're lucky... Yes!" A click, and a wavering beam lit up the wall. At once he swung the light up the stairs. Nobody was there.

"It must have been one of the other students," Nora said. "He looked a bit older than us."

"So where is he?" That was Bruce. "Evaporate?"

"Who knows?" Nora twitched a shoulder, carefully careless. "He could've walked out when we were messing around in the dark."

Jack tilted his head, listening. "He must have eyes like a cat, to come down here without a light."

"Or maybe," Bruce said in a creepy East European accent that Nora wouldn't have guessed him capable of, "maybe he is von off der children off der night...."

34

NORA PUT DOWN her treasured copy of *Dream Gold*. She couldn't concentrate on the story. Things she'd seen in the ruined prison, or thought she'd seen, kept crawling back into her mind.

"Skye?"

"Peace...." Skye was lying on her back on the other bed, hands crossed on her chest, eyes closed, breathing in through her nose and out through her mouth. "Peace...."

"Skye? You've been here a few days, right? You've seen all the other students."

"Mm-hm." Skye floated her hands up in the air.

"Which one is tall, longish hair, darkish, about eighteen..." Nora trailed off. That sounded so ordinary, and the boy on the stairs had been anything but. She closed her eyes and tried to recapture an image frozen in light for two seconds. It faded as she reached for it.

"There's one or two sort of like that," Skye said. "We'll scout them out tomorrow."

"I don't suppose you saw him? The boy on the stairs, I mean."

"Sorry, no." Skye floated her hands down and breathed.

Nora picked up her book, turned a page, and put it down again. She knew she'd sleep better once she'd convinced herself he'd been a real person and not some figment of her crazed imagination, like the inmates of those cells. I'm finished with all that, she told herself. No more stupid figments! I'm better now.

Something tickled her left eyebrow. She ran a hand through her bangs and a sky-blue blossom fell onto the quilt. It must have caught in her hair on the way into or out of the prison, or dropped from the vines that furred the prison wall. Darn things followed her everywhere!

She picked the flower off the bed and carried it to the window, a modern casement set in a sturdy old wooden frame. Pushing up the screen, she tossed the flower out into the night.

She stopped there for a moment to look up at the moon, full and silvery-bright in a cloudless indigo sky. Its face looked back at her encouragingly. The moon had not always been so benign. There had been a time when it made horrible faces at her. Not lately, though.

Then she went to her dresser and thoroughly brushed her hair.

STORM CLOUDS poured across the moon. The silver light dimmed, wavered, and died, plunging the garden into darkness. Nora stopped digging and rested where she knelt, braced on her hands, her white cotton pyjamas hiked over her knees.

All around her, invisibly, grass hissed and saplings thrashed. Bits of debris pattered on the stone wall. From somewhere near came the rhythmic soft roar of waves breaking on a stony beach.

When the moon tore free of the clouds and the garden sprang back into black and silver life, she started digging again. She had only her hands, but they were enough. She clawed up handful after handful of soft earth.

It bothered her that the hole never seemed to get any deeper, although she had been here for hours. Or was it years? Digging and digging, searching for the thing that was buried here. The thing she desperately had to find.

Her fingertips ran up against something hard just as the light failed again. *At last!* With a silent cry of triumph she yanked at it, pulling it free in a spray of dirt. The thing was long and thin, a stick of some kind, with a rounded shaft that felt like polished wood, one end narrower than the other, and cold metal at both ends.

The moonlight swelled again. She stood up and held out the stick to catch the moonlight. A hawk's head cast in yellow metal (gold? brass?) gleamed at the wider end. The hooked beak was sharp. A dark crystal eye glittered at her.

36

Strange, how clean it was. Not a smudge on it, not a crumb of dirt. You'd think it had just been polished.

Nora, came a silent voice.

She turned slowly, clutching the stick in both fists. He stood two long strides away. A tall boy, with the storm wind whipping dark hair back from a wide forehead. The moon gleamed on straight nose and high cheekbones, and picked out glints in the streaming hair.

An angel, she thought. A dark angel.

He stretched out his hand. *Mine.* His eyes were dark and hot.

No. How hard she'd worked to find this beautiful thing, how she'd blackened her hands for it!

And not only your hands.

She looked down at herself. The whole front of her pyjama, top and bottoms, was black with mud. Her feet were black and sticky. Or was it black? It had a reddish tint that was almost erased by the silver-blue moonlight. Mud, or....

Give it to me!

She slowly held the stick toward him. His face lit up. As his hand touched it and curled around the shaft, a fierce joy surged through the wood and into Nora's mind and body. She knew the joy was his.

SHE WOKE with a voice in her ears. The sound of her own name. *He knows my name, but I never told him.* And then she thought: *He knew it on the stairs, and I was awake then. I wasn't dreaming.*

She sat up in bed. Across the room, moonlight slanted in through the window. Wind stirred the curtain. No storm, no garden, no hawk-headed stick. No dark-haired boy.

And her pyjamas... she pushed back the quilt and looked.... were clean and white. Not mud-black or blood-red. Of course not.

Just a bad dream, and she was used to them. It meant nothing, nothing at all.

Chapter 7
Buried, Unburied

"THREE CIRCLES with radii of 3 cm, 4 cm, and 5 cm are touching each other as shown. A triangle is drawn connecting the three centres. Calculate all the interior angles of the triangle to the nearest degree." Jack groaned, dropped his pencil and sat back in his chair. "I don't know how we're expected to learn anything in these conditions," he muttered.

At the computer station next to him, Bruce stared at the screen and yawned. "It's an okay place. I guess."

"It's better than okay, that's the problem." Jack gazed out the window at the expanse of sparkling water and sunlit trees. Then he looked around the bright classroom, caught Dr. Beth's eye, and bent over Problem Number 11 again.

This island, in any sensibly run universe, was a place you came to swim and climb and hike, a place to soak up the sun and fresh air, not chain yourself to a textbook!

Worse, the view indoors was even better than the view outdoors. Across the table from him sat Nora, head on hand, daydreaming over a chemistry textbook. He knew she was daydreaming because she hadn't tapped a key on her computer more than once in the last half-hour. For most of the morning she'd been sketching instead of reading. Making little drawings in the margin of her notebook.

Dr. Beth had spoken to her about it twice already. The second time had been a long, earnest session at Dr. Beth's desk, out of Jack's hearing. Nora had come back pink and frowning, sat down, tore the

38

marked-up page out of her notebook and briskly started making notes on a fresh page. But soon her pen slowed, she gazed distantly past Jack's shoulder, and he knew she was off in dreamland again.

I'd give anything to know what she's thinking about. Except I'm pretty sure it isn't me, because I'm right here and she's hardly looked at me.

Dr. Beth cleared her throat and they both looked up, startled. She touched Nora on the shoulder. "I've put you down for extra tutoring with Cuthbert at four-thirty this afternoon. In the meantime, why don't you go for a walk?" She smiled. "Exercise can really freshen the mind."

Nora shot her a grateful look, grabbed up her books and was off, nearly running out the door. She turned right, toward the greenhouse and vegetable gardens. Funny! Jack stared after her. Wasn't she going to take her books back to her room?

"And now, Jack, maybe you can get some work done, too."

With his ears burning, he bent over his notebook again. Halfway through Problem 12, his restless foot brushed a paper on the floor, and he remembered the page Nora had torn out. He scuffed it closer with the toe of his sneaker, leaned over and picked it up, and smoothed out the crumpled page on the table in front of him.

Aside from a few scribbled notes and diagrams, the page was filled with little sketches of a bird's head — it looked like a hawk or falcon — and a dozen or more careful drawings of a human face. Pretty good drawings, too.

But an impossibly handsome face. Jack felt an odd, cold feeling inside, recognized it as disappointment, and tried to laugh at himself. Of course Nora would have a boyfriend! She was too pretty not to. This must be the guy she left at home. Arrogant-looking bastard. But maybe, he admitted, that was just sour grapes on his part.

He crumpled the page and tossed it aside. A moment later he

picked it up and smoothed it out again. Things clicked in his head. Why had Nora headed for the back of the house? Why in such a hurry? What about that guy she said she saw in the ruined jail yesterday?

He chewed his lip, then made a decision. Only one way to find out. But first... He ran an eye down the last three math problems, then got to work. Five minutes later he shoved back his chair and carried a handful of papers to Dr. Beth's desk.

"Finished! May I go now?"

"Just a moment." Her pencil moved down the pages, ticking off answers and hovering over demonstrations of method. Jack bobbed from foot to foot and glanced at the door.

"Hm." Dr. Beth's eyebrows went up. She sat back and gave him a smiling look. "So you can work — when you want to. We'll have to find something more challenging for you tomorrow!"

Jack sighed. He'd expected that. He grabbed his books and skedaddled.

Once outside, he turned right, the way Nora had gone. Stopping by the side of the greenhouse, he set his books down on an overturned crate — right beside the stack of Nora's books — and then ran on toward the log steps in the hillside.

Of course I could be completely wrong, he thought as he scrambled up the hill. But if I'm wrong she won't be there, and nobody will know what an idiot I'm being. On the other hand, if I'm right...

He slowed to a walk on the deer track that cut through the woods. *If I'm right, I'm an even bigger idiot. It's no business of mine where Nora goes or who she sees. Even if he does sneak around like a ferret.*

By the time the wall of the prison yard came in sight through the trees, Jack had almost talked himself out of chasing her. *If she's meeting some guy, she won't thank me for busting in. She might go off me altogether.*

He turned to head back. Then stood still on the path. *Only, I could have sworn she was scared of that place. Why would she go back there?*

Someone cried out, and he whipped around. It was someone in the prison yard. The cry came again, but by then Jack was halfway up the tree next to the wall.

"IT COULD HAVE been here," Nora told herself aloud. "Or was it here?"

She took another step and looked around, shaking her head. The trouble was, that spot in her dream could have been almost anywhere in the garden. She was sure of only one thing: it had been here inside these walls.

"But it had to be in an open spot, not right in among the trees, or I couldn't have been digging." Even as she turned slowly, searching, she was mentally cuffing herself. *Crazy! It was only a dream!*

All the same....

There was also this, that in her first hour on the island, here in this garden, she'd glimpsed somebody pacing, whacking at the grass with a stick. The two connected in her mind, the stick only heard and the stick only dreamed. She couldn't unlink them.

"I think it was over there." As she picked her way through the criss-crossing vines toward the prison wall, a sense of familiarity settled on her. In the dream, hadn't that big sapling been on her right?

She dropped to her knees and tried to clear a space among the blue-flowered vines. They grew so thickly here, close to the prison, their interlaced stems made a tough fabric. "You'd think — they were made — of iron!" She yanked with all her strength, and a vine broke and whipped back across her hand.

She gasped with pain. Then cried out as the broken vine curled

41

around her wrist.

Nora pulled free and jumped to her feet. One step, two, heading toward the prison. The spot in her dream had been closer to the wall, hadn't it?

Her foot caught in a snarl of stems. She staggered forward with a yell and sprawled on the ground.

This time, when she pushed up from the ground, it did her no good. She couldn't move her arms and legs. Then something green-and-blue flickered close to her eyes, and something cool slid across the back of her neck. A stealthy rustling sound was all around her.

The sunlight took on a greenish tinge. When she turned her head, she saw nothing but translucent green speckled with vibrant blue.

The vines! They're burying me!

"Nora?" Someone touched her shoulder. A warm human touch, this time. Now, suddenly, she could move. She sat up, brushing festoons of creepers from her arms and legs. They slid limply to the ground.

Jack sat on his heels, goggling at her as if she'd grown an extra head. "What the heck were you trying to do?"

"What did it look like?" She was on her feet now, stepping carefully to avoid getting snagged again. In a patch of grass that looked more or less vine-free, she stopped and sank down again. Her legs felt like wet spaghetti.

Jack flopped down beside her. "It looked like you were trying to dig a hole to China, face first."

She glanced at him sideways. What could she say that wouldn't sound crazy? She decided not to mention the vines. "Not quite that far. I had a really strange dream last night. I dreamt I was here, digging, and I found something."

She described the stick with the brass hawk's head. "I can still see every detail. It didn't fade, the way dreams usually do. It stayed stuck in my mind. Now, be honest." She turned so she could look straight at him. "If you had a dream as real as that, and it wouldn't let you alone, wouldn't you just have to go and look?"

"Okay, to be honest, yes, I would. But..."

"But what?"

"Was that all there was to the dream?"

"Well, there was someone..." No, I can't mention him. "Just some person," she finished lamely.

Jack looked away and shrugged, but she sensed she had disappointed him. "Anyway, there's obviously nothing here. It's just a sad, abandoned jail yard."

"You're right. Let's go." She climbed to her feet, then looked around at the towering walls. "I got in by way of the tree, but I never thought about how I'd get out again. Smart!"

"Piece of cake," Jack said casually. "Here's how I do it." A heavy branch, spiky with broken stems, lay close to the base of the vine-covered wall. It looked as if it had fallen from one of the taller pines outside. He heaved the top end up against the wall, then started climbing it.

"See," he twisted to call down over his shoulder, "it's a natural ladder. You can get high enough to grab the top of— Whoah!"

The branch slid sideways. Jack sprang free, hit the ground rolling, and fetched up flat on his back. Nora clapped her hands to her mouth, caught between laughter and alarm.

"Are you hurt?"

"Just my pride."

Nora laughed, then looked past him at the wall. "Jack! Look! Look what you've found!"

The sliding branch had torn a two-foot swatch of creepers from the wall. Nora stepped close and ran a hand over the surface of the exposed stones.

43

Jack was already beside her, pulling down more of the vines. Underneath was the shape of a doorway. Somebody had filled it in with fieldstone so that it looked almost like the rest of the wall. But the line of the arch, and the keystone in the centre, gave it away.

"You see, I was right! There was a gate!"

"Yes, but..." Jack picked at the rough grey mortar between the stones. "This wasn't filled in yesterday. I'd guess it's been like this for years. How could you have known about it?"

"I didn't know about it. Not like this. What I saw was different."

Standing in the sunlight, Nora shivered. So she hadn't been imagining things that didn't exist. Instead, she'd seen a gate that used to exist, a gate from another time.

What's happening to me?

Chapter 8

Blue-Eyed Invader

"JUST IN TIME for lunch. I could eat a woolly mammoth!" Jack led the way down the timber steps. Halfway down, he stopped and snuffled the air. "I just hope that isn't it!"

Nora sniffed. "Ew. Smells more like garden chemicals to me."

A pickup truck stood by the greenhouse. Hedda Shade, wearing thick gloves, was unloading two heavy sacks from the box and stacking them against the side of the building. A big orange KILL-X label was blazoned across each sack. Their pungent smell made Nora wrinkle her nose.

Dr. Cuthbert walked out of the greenhouse and waved at Jack and Nora as they came down the stairs. Then he spotted the sacks stacked beside the greenhouse, and stopped short. "Hedda, what are those?"

"Weed killer." She hefted one and balanced it on her shoulder. "For those weeds from the prison yard, the ones with the little blue flowers. They're getting out of hand."

"Haven't I told you we don't use chemicals here? We use natural methods wherever possible, Hedda."

"Well, natural methods don't work with these things, Dr. Loftus. They're too damn tough. And they're invasive as all get-out. They're even growing by the house now! D'you want them to overrun the whole island?"

He laughed gently. "I think that's hardly likely. Leave them alone, they're doing no harm."

She set her jaw, and for a moment Nora thought she was going to mouth off. Instead she turned abruptly, heaved up the sacks one by one, and dumped them back in the truck. Then climbed in and drove away, taking the gravel road toward the bridge. Cuthbert watched it disappear beyond a row of trees, his forehead more than usually furrowed.

Nora cleared her throat. "Um, Dr. Loftus? I think you should've listened to Hedda."

He looked at her in surprise. "Use chemicals? You should know better than that. I'd better raise the issue at our environmental studies seminar tomorrow."

"But I think she's right about those plants. I think they may be... um, poisonous."

"What makes you think that? Have you touched them?"

"Well, um, yes, it's hard not to, in, um..." She waved a hand. "In places. Where there's lots."

"Oh dear. Have they given you a rash? Let's see your hands."

She held out her hands and he bent over them, inspecting them back and front, and her arms, too. But of course there was no rash, nothing but a few scratches. She couldn't tell him the blue-flowered vines had attacked her, tried to drown her, tried to bury her. He'd think there was something wrong with her head if she came out with something like that. So would Jack, who was already looking at her oddly.

"They smell funny," she said. "And they make my eyes sting."

"Well, make sure you don't touch them, then. You may have a sensitivity." Cuthbert straightened up and smiled at her. "But, Nora, I've handled them, often, with my bare hands, and I haven't had a reaction of any kind. So have others. I suspect they're a variant of some quite common native wildflower: flax, or wild phlox, perhaps."

"Phlox! You're kidding! We have those at home." She felt at once, without knowing why, that giving the flowers a name made

46

them less strange. And made her less (she admitted it) afraid of them.

"I only suspect!" Dr. Cuthbert rubbed his nose, in him a sign of perplexity. "You can see the foliage is different, and so is the form and number of the petals. I sent photos and a sample to the experts at the Ministry of Natural Resources, but even they can't say exactly what we have. So our blue-eyed flowers must be quite rare." His face lit up. "Perhaps they're even a unique subspecies found only on this island. Wouldn't that be wonderful?"

"Yeah, way cool!" Jack said.

"Exactly! So do you really think I'd let Hedda wipe them out?"

"I guess not," Nora murmured.

"Don't look so troubled! They're harmless, I promise. Just play it safe and don't go picking any, understood? Now, don't forget about our tutoring session this afternoon!" He waved a friendly finger at her and began to turn away.

Jack stepped forward. "Dr. Loftus? About that prison yard. When was that door in the wall blocked off?"

Cuthbert's smile vanished. "How do you know about that?"

"We were exploring, and we saw it, just the shape of it."

"We had it filled in some years ago." He was suddenly cold and distant, not like himself at all. Nora poked Jack's arm, but he didn't get the warning.

"But why fill it in?"

"To discourage people from using the yard. It's not a wholesome place, Jack." His eyes through the thick lenses held a strange expression: anger, or pain. Now, if you'll excuse me." He strode into the greenhouse and closed the door.

Jack stared at the closed door. "Yikes. What did I say?"

"I don't know, but you can see it bothered him a lot, whatever it was. I guess that means I can't go back there."

"I guess not." Jack was annoyingly chipper.

"Of course, he didn't actually say it's off limits, did he?"

AS THEY WALKED along the north side of the house, Nora remembered what Hedda had said. *They're even growing by the house now.* She peered down at the narrow strip of ornamental garden bordering the brick wall. It bristled with rather scrubby-looking native plants and shrubs — Dr. Cuthbert didn't believe in encouraging foreign species — and here and there with ivy that meandered up the walls.

"Do you see any of those blue flowers along here?"

Jack looked. "No. Should I?"

"Yes, there!" She pointed. "There, see? Hedda was right!"

A slender green stem had thrust from the earth and was curling in among the ivy. The feathery leaves were so new they glistened.

Nora looked up, then counted the windows along the second floor. "One, two... Hey! That's my room up there! It's growing right under my window!"

"Aren't you taking this a bit too personally?" Jack was looking at her in a worried way.

"I found one of the flowers in my hair last night. I threw it out the window. It must have rooted."

"Well, I'm no gardener, but I don't see how it could have rooted that fast. The plant must have been here before you came. Nothing to do with you."

She took a deep, shaky breath. "Okay. Maybe I'm just a bit on edge."

"Who wouldn't be?" He sounded relieved. "It's the heat. Uh, what are you doing?"

She had dropped to her knees to get a good, close look at the plant. Had it moved? She thought it had, but there was no breeze. As she watched, holding her breath, the tip of the plant twisted slowly,

48

and a delicate tendril slid up around the ivy stem beside it. The plant was at least an inch higher than when she'd first looked at it.

"Did you see that?" She sat back and pointed a trembling finger.

"Wow, yeah." Jack was on his hands and knees beside her. "That thing grows like blazes!"

"This shouldn't be happening. It's not natural." Right in front of her the feathery vine uncurled and a flower bud unfolded. It moved... the thought trotted into her mind... moved like an animal, not a plant. Like a cat waking up and stretching.

It also moved the way the vines had moved in the jail garden. Relief flooded over her. "Not so crazy after all!" she said aloud.

"What?" Jack was nearly nose-to-nose with the newly opened blue flower. "This is so cool! I've never actually seen a plant growing before. It's just like one of those time-elapse films, a whole day in two minutes."

"Jack!" She pulled at his sleeve until he turned and looked at her. "Back in the jail garden, when you said it looked like I was digging a hole to China and I didn't explain? It was those vines. I fell into them and they just grew over me, lickety-split. I couldn't get up."

"Really?" He goggled. "That must've been scary!"

"You're not kidding! I didn't tell you because I thought... I thought you wouldn't believe me." She pointed. "But there's the proof, right there!"

"Yeah." He stared at the vine again. "Look, it's still growing. I wonder if they're space vines. Like, you know, triffids."

"Triffids never grew this fast. Anyway, whatever it is, I don't want it growing under my window and I'm getting rid of it, no matter what Dr. Cuth says."

She got a good grip on the stem close to the ground and pulled. She half expected it to struggle. But no, it came up easily, long threadlike roots beaded with crumbs of earth.

Jack inspected it, then poked at the spot where it had come up. "Looks like you got all of it."

They walked together to the recycling area behind the green-house. Nora bypassed the compost bin, stuffed the plant into a trash bag, and tied it off tightly. "There, that's the end of that!"

Chapter 9
Fly in Amber

AT THREE O'CLOCK classes ended. Everyone, including the most ambitious older students, were pried loose from their books and computers and shooed outside.

"Next on the agenda: sunshine, fresh air and exercise!" announced Dr. Cuthbert, standing in the meadow above the shore in an enormous, baggy pair of red-and white Canadian flag swim trunks. "Who's up for snorkeling?"

"Me," Bruce said.

"And me!" Jack waved both arms. "Nora, how about you?"

Me? Go under the water? She forced a smile and shook her head. "I'm not a strong swimmer."

"Oh, come on. It'll be fun!"

"Maybe next week."

Fifteen minutes later she sat on the warm planks at the end of the jetty in her new, never-yet-wetted jade-green bathing suit and wide-brimmed raffia hat, and watched as half a dozen of the others dipped and dove and splashed a few yards further out.

She felt guilty about lying to Jack about her swimming skills. She was a strong swimmer: but that hadn't helped her, last September.

The water's surface crinkled under the breeze and cast golden spangles over the sandy bottom. It would be cool in there, refreshing as a glass of iced ginger ale on a hot day like this. Ridiculous, babyish, her being so afraid of the water, after all this time.

Right. I'll do it. I'll go back in. No way I'll be scared off forever!

She dipped a foot into the water and instantly felt the weight of it pulling at her. All those miles of water waiting only a few strokes out. The cold depths beyond the golden shallows. The far, dark fathoms, with their wrecks and their dead....

She yanked her foot back onto the pier and sat clasping her knees.

Everyone was here, except Skye. Dr. Cuthbert was coaching the snorkelers. Dr. Beth was giving stroke lessons from the swim platform, twenty yards out from shore. Two pairs of students were paddling along the shore in two canoes.

The boy from the prison stairs wasn't here, either. Since breakfast this morning Nora had made sure she'd got a look at every single person on the island, including the kitchen and housekeeping staff. Nobody looked anything like him. She was beginning to think again that she'd imagined him.

Waking dreams. Figments. Sickness.

"Hey there! I've got news." Skye settled onto the planks beside her, looking like a fashion model in a skimpy and probably expensive black bikini. She had braided her long silver-blond hair and wore a wide-brimmed straw hat with a white silk veil wrapped around the crown and floating out behind.

"Hey yourself," Nora said, aiming for upbeat and aware she was missing the target. "What news?"

Skye fished a tube of sunscreen out of her straw bag and began anointing her legs. "I've been talking to Zoe again. Remember, the cook's helper?"

"Uh-huh. And?"

"Well, it's not exactly news. It's about what happened all those years ago. The triple tragedy? Zoe wasn't here at the time, but she learned this from the cook, Mrs. Duggan, who *was* here then and knows all the details."

"And?" Nora repeated patiently.

"So, there were these two boys and a girl. It was a love triangle, like I figured. The girl was stabbed to death."

Nora groaned softly and covered her eyes with her hands.

"And here's the kicker." Skye leaned over and whispered, although nobody else was near enough to hear. "Know who she was? Can you guess?"

Nora dropped her hands. "Just tell me, okay?"

"That girl who died all those years ago? She was the Loftuses' daughter."

"No way!"

"You bet. Her name was Ursula and she was sixteen, the same age as us."

"Oh, no! Poor Dr. Cuth! Poor Dr. Beth!"

"And guess where she was killed? In that jail yard!"

Nora stared at her in horror. Skye sat back and nodded solemnly. "They never found the murder weapon. But one of the boys hanged himself in the jail. That sounds like a confession, doesn't it?"

One in the jail yard. One in the jail. No wonder Dr. Cuth looked like that when Jack asked him about the filled-in gate. Not a wholesome place, he'd said, and he was right.

And she'd been there, in those places where they died. It was just too horrible. Nora stood up, tossed her hat behind her and stepped to the end of the pier.

"Wait!" Skye grabbed at her hand. "We have to talk this over!"

Nora shook her off and dove. The cool green-gold water swallowed her up. Down she speared to the sandy bottom, then levelled off and skimmed outward. The water deepened and cooled, but it was still clear and bright as the inside of a church on a sunny morning, with the light lancing through the surface and shimmering all around her.

It was heaven. It was what she'd been missing, what she used to be so good at. For a moment she floated, free as an otter in the sea or a gull in the air. All the dark thoughts that had attached themselves to her, all the horrors, all the terrible things she couldn't do anything about, they washed away, and there was only this cool beauty, this golden peace.

For a moment, maybe two, it lasted. Then memory grabbed her by the throat. She choked and panicked. Twisting around, she thrust herself upwards. And came face to face with the nameless boy from the staircase in the jail.

He looked different from the way she remembered him. Perhaps it was the underwater light that distorted his features and gave his skin that greenish-grey cast. He looked gaunt and ill. A ribbon of weed was tangled in his hair. But when she met his eyes, they glowed with warmth.

He mouthed words. She understood instantly.

Remember your dream, Nora.

How do you know about my dream?

He smiled. *I was there, wasn't I?*

He held out a hand and she reached for it. Their fingertips met. His fingers were cold and strong. His face suddenly glowed, as if her touch had fed him new life. His eyes shone the red-brown of a fox's fur. The dark hair rippling back from his high forehead glistened fine as silk.

She couldn't look away. She had never seen anything like him. Never met anyone like him.

Around them the light shifted from gold-shot green to blue-green and then to purplish blue. Finally to a dusky violet. As the light thickened and darkened Nora felt the cold closing in. Her body was growing heavy and flaccid.

She knew, in a distant way, that too much time had passed while

54

she floated underwater. She knew something was wrong. But the limp heaviness seemed to have spread to her mind.

His eyes and his smile held her like a fly in amber. She could not break free.

Chapter 10

A Glimpse of Weasel

FOR SOMEONE who wasn't a strong swimmer, that had been some classy dive — smooth and sure. Jack sat on the edge of the swim platform, kicking his rubber fins in the water, and watched the spot where Nora went in. He tried to calculate where she would surface, based on the trajectory of that dive.

Just about *there*, probably. About midway between the jetty and the swim platform. He fixed his eyes on the spot and got set to applaud soon as she broke the surface.

Ten seconds went by. Fifteen. Twenty. Jack stood up. Maybe the other side of the swim platform? He looked. Nope.

"Hey, did anybody see Nora come up?"

He looked around. Dr. Cuthbert was showing Bruce how to dip his mask. Dr. Beth was shouting encouragement at a student on the other side of the platform. Nobody had heard his question.

Thirty seconds.

Jack dove off the platform and headed for the pier at a fast crawl. Just short of the place where she'd gone in, he upended and plunged. At first he didn't see her. He turned, searching, and there she was, floating, arms and legs gleaming pale, dark hair floating like weed around her face, eyes wide open. His heart thumped.

As he reached for her, his hands sliced through a column of water that felt like the runoff from a glacier. The thought went into storage somewhere in the back of his mind. The rest of him was silently shouting Nora's name.

When they broke surface, his arms around her, she drew breath in a great gasp. That relieved the worst of his fears. Skye was leaning over the edge of the pier, looking frightened. Nora began to struggle. Jack concentrated on towing her to the beach and not letting go no matter how much she thrashed around.

They sprawled on the sand together. Jack wouldn't have minded staying like that for a while, but she pushed him away and sat up. She looked dazed and even whiter than usual. She was shuddering. Skye jumped down onto the sand and wrapped a beach towel around her shoulders.

"What the hell happened?" Jack was unaccountably furious, now that the crisis was over. "I thought you were drowning down there!"

She had trouble finding her voice, and when she did it was husky. "I was perfectly all right."

"Leave her alone." Skye crouched beside her and fended him off. "Don't bully her."

"Bully her! I was saving her life!" He pried off his flippers and hurled them at the pier.

Nora climbed to her feet and took a step. "Think I've had enough excitement for one day." She staggered in the soft sand. Jack jumped up and grabbed her arm.

"You're still scowling," she said. He was amazed to see she was smiling. "Jack, thank you."

"For what? Disturbing your underwater siesta?"

"For... caring." She went pink and turned away. She clutched the towel closer and started back toward the school. Skye picked up Nora's hat and went after her.

Feeling that he too had had enough excitement for one day, Jack picked up his flippers and headed back in the same direction. He was careful to keep enough distance between him and the two girls that he wouldn't appear to be following them.

He had just reached the place where the sandy beach feathered into soil and sprouted wiry grass, when the back of his neck went cold. He stopped dead. For that moment he was certain that someone, somewhere back of him, was staring at him with intense loathing.

He turned, not so fast as to seem nervous. The corner of his eye caught movement, someone sliding like a weasel below the surface of the water. When he got a direct look, nobody was there. He guessed if he went to investigate, the weasel would be gone.

He flipped a hand, careless and contemptuous, in case the weasel was watching. Then he turned and sauntered on his way. But his back stayed stiff until he was nearly at the school.

Which one of the students would be slinking around like that? He thought back, and shook his head. It wasn't one of the students. He could account for every one of them.

But there was a village on the mainland, not far away. Three, four kilometres at most. A place called Serenity. This weasel had to be some guy from the village, come sliding over here to bother the girls.

Jack made a mental note to mention this to Dr. Cuthbert. And not to mention it to Nora. He didn't want to scare her.

WITH HIS LONGER LEGS, Jack caught up to Nora and Skye as they reached the side door of the school. They walked in single file along the corridor toward the front of the house.

A door on the right opened as Skye passed, and Hedda Shade stepped out. She stopped in the doorway, hand on knob, to let them go by. Nora glanced at her, then looked beyond her, and stopped so suddenly that Jack walked into her.

She didn't seem to notice. She was staring over Hedda's shoulder at something in the room. For a long moment the four of them held a frozen tableau. Then Nora said, "Who's that?" Her hand rose, shaking.

58

Jack looked where she was pointing. On the opposite wall of the room, large enough to be clearly visible from here, hung an enlarged photograph of a boy a little older than himself.

He was sure he'd never seen this guy before. Or wait, maybe he had. In a drawing on the edge of a notebook page. It was a face you'd remember — with intense dislike, he thought. Handsome, arrogant, the centre of his own universe. Jack wasn't sure how he could read all that from this distance, but he could.

"Who's that?" Nora repeated, louder, more intense.

Hedda gazed at her with a strange, hungry look. Then her face hardened. "That's my son, Adam." She stepped back inside and slammed the door.

Nora backed away, still staring at the door. "That was him!" she hissed.

"Who?" Skye demanded. Jack had already guessed.

"The boy who...." Nora looked nervously at Hedda's door. "Not here." She led the way along the corridor to the lobby. The only sound in the house was a clink of pots in the kitchen wing, and the drone of a vacuum cleaner upstairs.

At the bottom of the stairs Nora stopped, turned around, and took a deep breath. "That was the boy I saw in the prison last night. I saw him again, just now, when I was swimming."

"Swimming?" Skye looked baffled. "But I was there. Why didn't I see him?"

"Because when I saw him, it was under water."

"That's weird!"

"You bet it is," Jack said. "But I think I saw him too, as I was leaving the beach. Just a glimpse."

Nora took another deep breath. "You might as well have the whole story. I've seen him one other time. In a dream."

Skye smiled knowingly. "Oh, well..."

"And he knew about the dream."

"Oh." Skye's eyes widened. "That's different. In fact, it could be very important. Come upstairs and tell me every detail you can remember."

She linked her arm in Nora's and the two girls started up the stairs. Knowing he'd been elbowed aside yet again, Jack ran up after them and stopped Nora with a touch on her towel-draped arm.

"Nora, will you promise me something? Be careful of this guy, will you?"

She looked as if she wasn't sure whether to laugh at him or slap him. "I don't need a big brother, thanks so much!"

"Besides, Jack, you don't know a thing about him," Skye put in. "You haven't even met him!"

"No, and I don't think I'm likely to, either, not when his game plan is skulking around where he can catch girls alone! I wouldn't trust this Adam Shade as far as I can throw him."

Chapter 11

Dowsing

NORA AND SKYE had their heads together through dinner. They're planning something, Jack thought. What were they up to? Not that it was any of his business.

Unless I make it my business.

He spent half an hour pacing in his room, fighting the urge to go and find Nora and talk sense into her. Something — whether it was that half-glimpsed slither of movement, or the touch of loathing eyes on the back of his neck, a touch he could still feel — had convinced him this Adam was not somebody Nora should be mixing with.

She'll just laugh at you, said his sensible side. Or worse, she'll get mad, and then she won't listen to you.

But somebody's got to look out for her, his instinctive side insisted. That somebody sure won't be Skye. She has about as much common sense as a flying squirrel.

By seven-thirty his instinctive side won the debate and he went looking for her. She wasn't anywhere inside the school, or swimming, or bending over a row in the vegetable garden. He found Bruce behind the garden, tossing a football to one of the younger students.

"Bruce, have you seen Nora?"

"Uh-huh." Bruce caught the football with a smack. "A minute ago." He hurled the ball.

"Where?"

"Going up the hill." He jerked his head at the timber steps. "With Skye."

"Yeah? Were they carrying anything?"

"Spade. Shears."

Jack was quick off the mark. He caught up with them just as they reached the deer track. They heard him coming and looked back. Nora was wearing khaki shorts and a T-shirt, and carrying a spade. Skye was dressed in a flowing, lacy white dress and carrying a large pair of garden shears. A small black velvet bag hung from one wrist. She had painted her nails pale green, with silver stars.

"You look like a Christmas tree ornament," Jack commented. "Easy to see who's going to be doing all the dirty work."

Skye tossed back her hair. "Don't you ever know when you're not welcome?"

"Wait a minute." Nora put a hand on her arm. "He is welcome. That is, so long as he doesn't try to stop me. It's just something I have to do, Jack, or I won't sleep."

"Or get much studying done?"

"That too." She smiled lopsidedly. "I need to find that thing that I saw in my dream. If I can do that, I'll find Adam — somehow — and get him to explain everything. There has to be a rational explanation, doesn't there? I mean, even for things that seem incredible at first."

"So I always used to think." He was remembering the filled-in gate in the wall, and he knew she was too. But that didn't change what he had to do now. "Wait here," he said. "Give me ten minutes. That's all I ask."

JACK CAME BACK with a second spade and an extra pair of hands. Bruce was lugging a leather backpack that sagged and clanked when he moved. A long steel bar jutted up above his shoulder.

Skye and Nora were still there, waiting: Skye standing with arms crossed impatiently, Nora perched on a rock beside the path. She stood up when the boys came in sight. Judging by the relieved look on Jack's face, he hadn't expected them to wait.

Jack reached into the backpack and handed Nora a sturdy flashlight. "You'll want this inside the building. We've got four of them."

She shoved it back at him. "I'm not going back inside that place ever again!"

"Then how did you plan to get over the wall, you with your shovel and Skye in that fancy dress?"

Nora looked at Skye, who quirked an eyebrow. "He's got a point. It would be easier going through the building."

"But you said the inside door to the garden was nailed shut." Nora looked at Jack.

"That's what the crowbar's for."

She made a face, then nodded, and hoped they couldn't guess how frightened she was. "Where'd you get all this stuff?"

"Borrowed the spades from the garden shed, the crowbar from the back of the pickup, and the flashlights from the furnace room."

"Borrowed?"

"Well, liberated. Okay, stole. Now, don't look like that! It's temporary. Everything will go back where it came from."

"It better, or we're all in trouble," Skye said.

As they picked their way along the narrow track, Nora shielded her eyes against flickering gleams of sunlight. The sun's angle was reassuring. There was more than an hour yet until sunset. Plenty of time for what she had to do. She hoped.

When they reached the cliff top overlooking the bay, a sound like kettle drums rolled across the water. Nora squinted against the light. A purple band of cloud was puffing up into towers above the horizon.

"It's going to storm." She wavered between relief and disappointment.

"Call it off?" Jack asked casually.

She hesitated, then raised her chin. "No. But let's hurry."

"That storm is miles and miles away," Skye said. "We'll be snug in bed by the time it gets here."

After leaving the prison last night, Jack had laid the planks across the broken door and tapped a few of the nails back in. Now he pulled them off again. Reaching into the backpack, he handed out flashlights.

Then, with an encouraging grin at Nora, he ducked under the slanted door. Skye went next, carefully holding her white dress away from the splintery doorframe. Then Bruce, and finally Nora.

It wasn't as bad as last time, she told herself, as they walked through the entrance room, their four flashlights shining this way and that. Dust, and cobwebs, and the cold, unwholesome smell of a place that had never been happy and had been abandoned for years. That was all.

She focused on the back of Bruce's T-shirt as he walked ahead of her through a steel-framed doorway on the right side of the room and along a corridor lined with cell bars. No hands came drifting to the bars, no feet scraped on the gritty floor inside the cells. Of course not.

Only misery welling up from below like black water, and a far, faint, windy sound that might be voices. *Help us, help us....*

"No. It isn't real."

"What?" Bruce looked back.

"Nothing."

They found another steel door at the end of the corridor. It was criss-crossed with planks. Jack pulled the crowbar from Bruce's backpack and handed it to him. As Bruce ripped off the planks, Jack caught each one and tossed it aside. In a couple of minutes the door was free.

"Might have to jimmy this too," Jack said as he wrenched at the handle.

But the door screeched open, and Nora saw that the lock had

been violently smashed. She wondered who had done it, who had felt that way. Then, as she followed the others out into the garden, she thought only of taking deep, cleansing breaths of the moist evening air.

Skye kicked off her sandals, then opened her velvet bag and slid out the rose quartz pendant. She began pacing, slowly and with dignity, barefoot through the ferns and creepers, holding the pendant out at arm's length ahead of her.

Jack watched incredulously, then raised his arched eyebrows at Nora. "What the hell does she think she's doing?"

"Skye's testing the aura of the prison yard. She thinks it may be diseased. Also, she's looking for a wand."

"A wand," he said flatly.

"For dowsing."

"Dowsing!" He laughed. "Nora, I thought you were too smart for this kind of codswallop!"

She flushed, because he'd put her own thoughts into words. But she had to defend Skye. "It isn't codswallop, whatever that is. It's just... well, it's things that haven't been proven, but might be true. And anything's worth a try, right?"

Inside the high walls, evening had fallen. It was drowsy in here, heat still radiating from the stones, the tall grass and saplings hardly stirring, the buttercups closed tight.

But everywhere the blue-eyed flowers were awake, looking out from the shadows near the walls. Nora caught a flicker of movement, thousands of eyes turning in her direction.

"Let's do it now," she said urgently. "We can't stay here all night."

"Well, of course we can't!" Skye came back holding a forked branch by its midsection. "Look, Nora, this is perfect. Mountain ash."

"Dowsing?" Jack repeated, as if he still couldn't believe his ears.

65

"Why not something that actually works, like a metal detector?"

"Because we haven't got a metal detector," Skye said coldly. "Unless you've got one in your backpack, there. Do you?"

"Ah, no."

"No. And dowsing does work. Hand me your pocket knife."

She tucked the pendant into its velvet bag and hung the bag by its cord over her wrist. Jack reluctantly got out his cool device, unfolded a blade and handed it over, and she began slicing extra twigs and leaves from the forked branch.

Bruce's eyebrows lifted, for him the equivalent of a shout of surprise. "We're prospecting for water?"

Skye laughed. "That shows how much you know. Dowsing's been used for thousands of years to find missing bodies, and minerals, and even bombs. Yes, and water too." She slashed as she talked. "Modern oil companies use dowsers to find oil, for heaven's sake! How much more proof do you want?"

Bruce said nothing. Jack threw his hands in the air. Skye smiled and examined her peeled wand. It gleamed like ivory. Then she held it out to Nora. "Just for fun, why don't you have first go at it?"

It occurred to Nora that Skye might be a tad less confident than she made herself out to be about this dowsing experiment. She looked at the others, but Bruce had settled on the ground against the backpack, and Jack was smiling sceptically, hands deep in pockets.

"Sure, why not?" Nora poked her flashlight into the backpack and got a good grip on the forked ends of the stick. The peeled wood was slightly sticky. She tried to remember what Skye had told her. Closing her eyes, she held out the stick level with the ground and took a slow step. Then another.

"Um... nothing's happening."

"Maybe you've got no talent," Skye said. "Do it a bit more, then I'll try."

"I don't think there's much point..." Nora's voice trailed off. The oddest feeling was trickling into her hands. It was like pins and needles, only there was movement in it. Fainter now, fading... No, getting stronger. "S-something's happening."

"Nora?" Jack's voice. She shut it out. This was real, not something she'd imagined. This was a known thing, a natural and wholesome power.

With her eyes closed she pictured it flowing up out of the ground, through the wood, into her hands. The life of the earth: the hidden springs, the deep roots. Its flow was an intertwining of pale blue and green glowing threads, fresh and delicate as the first shoots of spring.

Faster and fuller it flowed, a stream of power, cool and clean. In one corner of her mind Nora stood back and gaped in disbelief. The rest of her rejoiced in what was happening. She felt strong and sure and free of self-doubt for the first time in nearly a year.

Then the feeling changed. First, a sudden nausea in the pit of her stomach. Then the blue-green threads dimmed and darkened. A murky crimson stain spread through the wood and into her hands, and with it came a horror so intense that she screamed and flung the stick away.

When she lifted her hands, they were dripping with blood.

Chapter 12

Treasure Trove

"NORA! WHAT'S WRONG? Did you hurt yourself?"

Jack was holding her by the shoulders. She pushed him away and looked at her hands again. They were clean, not a mark on them, but they fluttered like aspen leaves. She hid them in her shorts pockets.

"I'm all right."

"But you acted like something stung you! And you're as white as a ghost."

Skye was bouncing with excitement. "You felt something! Didn't you?"

"Yeah. I did. But it wasn't something good. I wonder if maybe we should call this off."

"What! After finding out it really works? Let me try it!"

Bruce had made himself useful by searching among the grass and wildflowers until he found the ash wand. He handed it back to Skye. She gripped it gingerly by the forks, set her teeth and began walking slowly back and forth. After a moment she stopped, frowned, shifted her grip, and tried again. A few minutes more, while the others watched impatiently. Finally she sighed and handed the stick back to Nora.

"Nothing. Not a glimmer."

Nora was about to throw the thing away, when Bruce unexpectedly took it from her hands. "Let me have a go."

Skye snorted, but he ignored her. He stood for two minutes holding the stick, slowly turning in a circle, scowling in concentration. "Nope," he said at last. "Your go." He tossed the stick to Jack, who flinched as he caught it, as if it might bite him.

Then he grinned and gave himself a shake. "Why not? It can't hurt. Might as well pick up where Nora left off." He took up a position in the place where she'd been standing. Then he gripped the wand firmly and held it out parallel to the ground. None of them moved. Nora held her breath. Maybe it wouldn't work for him either, maybe you had to have a gift. Or a curse....

The stick twitched in his hands. His eyes opened wide. He nearly dropped it, then gripped more tightly. "Omigosh!"

"What's it feel like?" Skye hovered at his elbow.

"It's incredible! It's like — it's like I've got a big dog on a leash!" His arms were trembling with strain, his knuckles white. He closed his eyes and started walking slowly across the yard.

"Watch out, man," Bruce warned. Jack's foot snagged in a tangle of creepers and he staggered, but Bruce caught him by the arm. Jack still had his eyes squeezed shut. He took another step. And another, and another. Straight across the yard toward the wall of the prison.

The nearer he came to the wall, the stronger the pull. You could see it in the strain on his face, the sweat dripping down his cheeks, the knots in his arms. "Pulling — down — now."

Suddenly he gasped and let go, and the wand speared down.

"Couldn't hold it!"

"You're about as far as you can go, anyway," Skye said.

Jack was standing knee-high in a tangle of the blue-flowered vines, next to the wall of the prison, about five strides away from the steel door. A large maple sapling grew nearby. Just like in my dream, Nora thought.

In fact, this was the very spot where the vines had tried to trap her this morning. Now that she'd had a good look at the garden, it was obvious there were more of them in this place than anywhere else. They were climbing all over the prison wall, here. Yet they didn't seem to be hampering Jack or Bruce.

Jack mopped his face with the sleeve of his T-shirt and flashed a grin at Nora. Then sketched a bow to Skye. "Apologies. You were right and I was wrong."

She lifted hands and eyes. "Well, the sky has fallen!"

The kettledrums boomed again, nearer. Bruce glanced at the sky, then picked up a spade. "Let's do it."

Jack picked up the second spade. Seeing Nora, he smiled. "Don't look so worried! If it's here, we'll find it."

"Just a minute." She took the shears and used them to chop through the vines where Jack was standing. A strong, bitter odour rose from the cut stems. She set her mouth, steeled herself, and pulled aside thick sheets of the interwoven creepers.

The exposed earth beneath was damp and dark, and looked unclean. The dowsing wand stuck up from the centre of the bared patch. It had sunk into the earth right up to the fork. Skye pulled it out and gingerly laid it aside.

Jack took up a position facing Bruce, both of them side-on to the wall. He sank his spade into the earth and scooped. Nora's stomach tightened. Bruce heaved up the second spadeful while Jack was tossing his aside, then Jack's spade bit.

"That's it — like a well-oiled machine," Jack said with a laugh, and started digging furiously. Nora stood staring at him. Since he'd taken hold of the wand, there'd been an extra exuberance in him, an edge of wildness. She wasn't sure she knew him any more.

Skye stood back beyond the shower of dirt. "Nora? When you held it, what did you feel?"

"Whatever it was, it must've been different from what Jack felt. He seems okay. I think."

"Well, this is an old prison. Lots of bad karma must have got dumped here. You obviously tapped into one of the bad spots, while he found one of the good ones."

"You said..." Nora rubbed her arms. "You said Ursula was killed here. Maybe that's why I...." She swallowed. "I saw blood all over the wand. All over my hands."

Skye sucked in her breath and they edged closer together. There was some comfort in that. Nora was glad she wasn't here alone. Although, she thought, if the red-stained horror that was still lurking at the back of her mind were to take a shape they could all see, Skye wouldn't be much protection. Nor Jack nor Bruce. Nothing could protect you against something like that.

The spades bit, tossed, bit again. The diggers gasped with effort, even Bruce. Jack's white T-shirt was grey with sweat and dirt. Nora realized the garden was grey as well, with dusk. Not true night, but storm-dusk.

Thunder growled, nearer. "Look there!" Nora pointed. Top-heavy clouds, coloured like bruises, had swallowed the sun. The trees around the garden turned from gold to black, and suddenly bowed low. The gust tore Nora's hair.

"It's going to storm like crazy!" Skye said.

"You're right. We can't do this now." Nora felt light with relief. "Jack! Time to call it off!"

"Not now! We're close! Got to be!" He was standing in the hole, his bare legs and arms black with dirt. "We're already three feet down."

"Well, you're going to be wallowing in mud, any minute now!" Skye said. "And you won't even be able to see. Bruce, tell him not to be stupid."

"Not my call." Bruce scooped out another spadeful.

"Look, I'll prove we're close." Jack crawled out of the hole and grabbed the ash wand. As soon as his hands were in place on the

71

forked ends it jerked forward and down. With a yell he fell to his knees, still hanging on to the wand.

"Look! It's trying to go forward, not down," Skye said. "That doesn't make any sense."

"It's trying to go forward *and* down." Jack let go of the stick and for a moment it stayed up by itself, the sharp wooden snout burrowing like a beetle at the stones of the jail's foundation. Then it toppled, lifeless. Bruce picked it up and tossed it carelessly onto the heap of cut vines. Nora stared at it in horror.

"You know what this means." Jack took his spade and knocked it against the wall. It was built of rough fieldstone like the rest of the building and the wall of the prison yard, and gave back a solid clunk.

"But it can't be inside the wall!" Nora protested.

"Why not? Best place in the world to hide something. Who'd ever find it?"

Wind whipped Nora's hair into her eyes and blew out Skye's pale mane like a banner. Like my dream, she thought. A drop of rain hit Jack's cheek. He ignored it, crawled to his backpack, pulled out the crowbar and slid back into the hole. He started chipping at the mortar between the stones.

No!

Nora's head went up. "Who said that?"

"Who said what?" Skye looked around. Nora shook her head.

Rain laced the wind now, lashing their arms and faces. "Almost — got it!" Jack heaved with all his strength. The stone broke free and toppled into the mud, just missing his toes. They all leaned forward. Behind it lay...

More stones. Nora let her breath out.

Jack handed the crowbar to Bruce. "Here, get some exercise. Try lower down, this time."

Bruce worked his shoulders to get the kinks out, then started methodically digging at the foundation. Thunder rumbled overhead. The rain was pelting down now, plastering their clothes to their bodies. The wind ripped at their hair. Jack crouched in the mud, watching intently. Even Skye was focused so tightly on what Bruce was doing, she didn't notice that her hair and dress were soaked.

Another stone rolled out. "Think there's a bit of a gap behind there," Bruce said.

"Yes!" Jack punched at the sky in triumph. A crack of thunder answered him. Nora gasped.

"There *is* someone calling!" She strained to hear. Was it *Nora, Nora* or was it *No... no...*

The next stone that Bruce pried loose left a patch of darkness behind. Jack knelt with his face nearly in the mud to get a look inside. Then he turned his head and yelled, "Flashlight!"

Slipping in the wet grass, Skye ran to bring it to him. He poked the light in and went dead still. Then he sat back on his heels. "Found it," he said, quiet and gleeful.

Nora went cold.

"What?" Skye squealed. "What did you see?"

"It's a big cavity, and there's something in there."

"Leave it like that," Nora said impulsively. "Don't disturb it!" But the wind blew her words away. Already Bruce was at work with the crowbar, while Jack scraped more dirt from the base of the wall. She told herself not to be stupid. Here it was, the thing she'd set out to find: the thing that would prove she wasn't crazy, that all these things were not just bits of dreams.

Just as the hole became big enough to let them all look inside, a stone broke free from the top of the cavity and thudded into the ground an inch from Bruce's foot. "Hey!" He looked up. "I don't like the looks of that."

Even in the storm-dark you could see cracks in the mortar around

73

two or three more stones at the top of the hole.

"Okay, knock them down," Jack said casually. "The rest of the wall's fine." He swung his spade and the stones fell with a shower of mortar. Then he picked up the flashlight and waved it. "Nora, you should be over here. This is your big moment. All your idea, remember?"

Skye crouched down at the edge of the hole. Nora knelt beside her, fingers digging into the mud. All four flashlight beams shone through the silver lines of the rain into a cavity about three feet long and six inches high. The light wavered over a tattered shape. The boom of thunder and the whistle of wind faded to the back of Nora's attention.

Jack reached in and lifted the shape from its hiding place. The cloth covering was crusty and dry. He peeled it away and let it drop. Across his two hands lay a long shape that gleamed in a sudden flash of lightning.

Not even dusty. Shining as if it had just been polished. So I was right, Nora thought. Then, *We should put the thing back right now, close it up, bury it.* She opened her mouth to say so, but her lips were too stiff to form words.

Jack turned the stick to and fro, and the hawk's crystal eye glittered at them. "Beauty," he murmured. "Here, Nora, take it. You were right. I just don't know how you knew."

As he turned to offer it to her, the stick slipped in his grip. He hissed in pain. Blood welled from a long cut across the back of his left hand. He dropped the stick, but Bruce caught it before it could touch ground and handed it to Nora.

"Watch out for that beak, it's sharp," he said matter-of-factly.

That was the moment everything came apart.

Another stone fell from the top of the cavity. At the same instant a huge figure loomed up behind them, terrifying in a sudden flare of

74

lightning.

"You kids! What on earth are you — Oh my God."

Next moment Cuthbert was down in the hole, yelling, shoving Bruce up and out as if he weighed nothing. "Get out! Move! Can't you see it's going to collapse?" He grabbed Jack by an arm and the back of his shorts and tossed him up onto the grass.

Then, with a roar that shook the ground under Nora's feet, the wall of the prison disintegrated. Cuthbert went down beneath it.

Chapter 13

Deadly Secrets

"I WONDER if you understand, all of you, just what you've done?"

Jack tried to meet Beth's eyes, but didn't quite make it. She stood braced against a desk in her office, as if she needed its help to stay upright. She looked pale, greyer and older after a sleepless night at the West Parry Sound Health Centre.

Of the five people in the room, only Bruce had slept much, that was obvious. Jack had lain awake all night listening to him snore. In the colourless light that sidled through the rain-washed windows this morning, almost every face looked pale and tired. Nora's eyes were big and dark, underscored with purple smudges.

Jack cleared his throat. "He is going to get better, isn't he? He, he won't...."

There it was, the fear none of them had been able to put into words. That Cuthbert would die. That they would have killed him.

No, that I would have killed him. All my fault.

Beth drew a breath and closed her eyes briefly. "He'll recover. He has a nasty concussion and some broken bones and bad bruising. But nothing that won't mend, given time."

Nora knotted her hands together. "It was my idea—"

Beth held up both hands. "I'm not assigning blame. I know none of you meant any harm. But consider what happened because of your escapade," she went on evenly. "Not only was Cuthbert badly hurt, but the school has been disrupted. Eight other students besides your-selves have been deprived of a teacher. Lessons have had to be can-

76

celled. I'll need to hire someone to take Cuthbert's classes, at short notice." Her eyes moved from face to face. "I want you all to promise me you'll think about that."

"I will." "Oh, yes." "Yes, of course," they chorused. Bruce ducked his head and mumbled something.

"And I hope you'll all be using your creative energies more constructively in future. Today's classes will start after lunch, or as soon as the supply teacher can get here. Until then, you're dismissed."

"I feel incredibly guilty," Jack muttered to Nora as they filed out of the study and walked slowly along the corridor toward the lobby.

"So do I."

"You?" He stared. "Why should you feel guilty? I was the one who bulled ahead, when you kept saying no, we should quit. If it wasn't for me, we wouldn't have damaged the wall, and Dr. Cuth wouldn't have been hurt."

"And I had the big idea about dowsing," Skye muttered. "Which worked great, but maybe not the way we wanted."

"But I started the whole thing." Nora set her teeth. "And then I knew something terrible was going to happen. I knew it and I should have found a way to stop it!"

"How?" Bruce put in. "The only way you could've stopped Jack last night would've been to tie him in a sack." Without another word he turned and marched out the front door.

Jack hunched his shoulders but didn't reach for a smart answer, because Bruce was right. "I couldn't think of anything except finding it. Finding what was buried there. It seemed like the most important thing in the world. But now that I look back..." He frowned at the black-and-white floor. "It was weird. I wasn't thinking straight."

"You weren't the only one," Nora said. "I almost felt as if there were other people in the garden with us. One side trying to force us one way, the other side trying to force us the other way. And us

77

caught in the middle."

"I didn't sense anything like that." Skye tapped Nora's arm. "But now that Jack's mentioned what was buried there, how about it? We never got a good look at it. You didn't lose it?"

"Of course not, I put it away safe." Nora seemed reluctant, but when Skye kept looking at her expectantly, she nodded glumly and went upstairs. When she came down again she was holding something long and thin wrapped in a T-shirt.

"Let's take it outside, where the light is better," Skye said eagerly.

As they stepped out of the front door, they found the rain had stopped. The sun broke through the flying clouds and pulled sheets of mist up from the soaked forest. The island steamed like a big soup pot.

Nora wouldn't unwrap the thing until they were halfway down the road toward the bridge, and the school was hidden around the bend behind. Then she stopped and let the folds of cloth fall away from the cane.

Jack whistled softly. It really was a beautiful thing. A two-foot length of polished wood, mahogany maybe, with a rich red-brown colour and a grain pattern like eddying water. The foot, at the smaller end, was covered with a brass cap. The top end was encased in a collar of the same metal, about a hand's width wide, below the falcon's head. That head was the really amazing part, he thought. The crystal eyes made it look fiercely alive.

"Now isn't that funny," Skye said. "You'd think it would be all rusted and rotten."

"Obviously somebody went to a lot of trouble to keep it dry. Oiled it, probably." He grasped the stick by the collared end, below the hawk's head — carefully, mindful of the bandaged cut on the back of his left hand — and swished it experimentally through the air. Then poked it toward the ground. "Too short for a walking stick. What's it for?"

"Just for show, I guess," Nora said. "I think rich men used to carry them."

"But why bury it?" That was the thing that was bothering Jack. "It's a real nice cane, but why go to all that trouble to hide it?"

Nora looked at it warily. He noticed that she hadn't touched it any more than she had to, and not with her bare hands. "It must have meant something important to somebody."

He knew she was thinking of her dream, and the boy who might or might not be Adam Shade. Who had not yet turned up to answer questions. Like, how he managed to get into her dreams.

"So, now what do we do with— Oh, no! I've broken it!"

The brass collar loosened in his grip. It was more than loose, it was sliding right off, hawk's head included, and bringing with it a strip of metal from inside the shaft. He pulled it all the way out and gasped.

The sun flashed off a steel blade. Jack measured it with his eyes. A good eighteen inches long. An inch wide where it was set in the collar, and gradually narrowing to a needle-like point. He turned it back and forth to catch the sun. Both edges glittered razor-sharp. "Wow, beauty!"

"Are you kidding? It's terrifying!" Nora backed away.

"Well, yeah. Beautiful and scary, both at the same time. That would really keep you safe in the back alleys, eh?"

"Careful, don't wave it around." Skye grabbed Nora's arm.

"Put it away, Jack, please!"

He would have liked to try a few lunges and parries. But to please her, and because she looked so upset, he slid the blade back into the stick. The brass collar clicked sweetly into place, and the join felt solid again.

Nora relaxed, now that the blade was out of sight. "We've got to find out more about it. But who could we ask?"

"Well, Beth..." Jack began, then the three exchanged looks and shook their heads. Best not to bother Beth about anything found in that garden.

"There's a funny little man in the village who might help," Skye said. "He runs a really neat store with lots of old, interesting stuff. Old books, antique jewellery, things like that. One of the other students told me about it and I went there a couple of days ago."

"Worth a try," Nora said.

Jack glanced at his watch. "If we start now and walk fast, we can get there and back by lunchtime."

Chapter 14
The Golden Snake

ISAAC FREY, BOOKSELLER AND ANTIQUARIAN, said the sign over the door, in slightly crooked hand-painted gold letters. The shop was a one-storey fieldstone cottage with a sharp central peak and pointed gothic windows. Jack pulled open the door, setting a string of brass bells jangling.

At first they thought the shop was empty. The front room, which took up the full width of the cottage, was crammed from plank floor to beamed ceiling with odds and end of furniture, cabinets displaying tarnished spoons and mismatched cups and saucers, and shelves of mildew-spotted books. More books were stacked in the corners.

On a chest-high wood-panelled counter with a glass top stood an ornate brass cash register that had to be an antique itself. Unexpectedly (at least it surprised Jack), a life-sized plaster statue of Venus stood beside the counter, wearing a dusty top hat and nothing else.

As the jangle of the bells died away, a small figure stepped from behind the counter. "Hello!" he said to Skye. "Couldn't stay away, I see!"

Jack stared. He had formed a mental picture of the antiquarian: a tiny, shrivelled gnomelike creature, bent under the weight of years. The reality was different. Isaac Frey was small — shorter even than Nora — but not tiny, and not ancient. Probably not out of his twenties, Jack guessed. His badly cut hair was a blazing red. He bounced when he walked. The only nod to his role as antiquarian was a long, old-fashioned black coat, worn open over a Blue Rodeo T-shirt, jeans and sneakers. He saw Jack looking at it and smoothed the silk lapels.

"Frock coat. Height of style in 1880," he said. "And now, what can I do for you? Want some cool adventure books? Tom Swift? How about a game of Snakes and Ladders?" He darted from shelf to counter, gathering books and boxes. "Victorian rings for the ladies? Genuine abalone shell, I guarantee it."

Jack felt a little breathless, watching him. Skye giggled. "Actually, Mr. Frey, we're not here to buy."

"Hey, it's Ike. Nobody misters me!" He waggled his reddish eyebrows up and down. "But if you're not planning to part with any cash, may I ask why...."

"We need your advice," Nora said firmly. She placed the rolled-up T-shirt on the counter beside the cash register and unwrapped it.

Ike went suddenly quiet. He shaped a silent whistle, and ran an admiring finger along the wood stock, before delicately picking up the cane with the fingertips of both hands. "Now, this is a real nice piece of Victoriana, unless I've completely lost my touch. I wonder, is it..."

He grasped the brass collar, twisted, and drew out the blade. "Yes, it is!" he crowed. "Lovely, lethal thing. But where on earth did you get it? Don't tell me you kids routinely bring sword sticks to summer school!"

Nora exchanged a worried look with Jack. She studied Ike's face a moment and then seemed to make up her mind. "You know the old prison? On the island? We found this buried in the jail yard."

"Buried?" He stared at them in amazement. "I'll bet there's a story there. You didn't just stumble on it."

"No, I..." Nora bit her lip, then gave him an edited version of how they'd found the stick. She didn't mention dreams.

"Dowsing! Pull the other." He grinned at her. "That wasn't the whole story, was it? Never mind. You know what I think? I think that stick belonged to Governor Garvey. Heard of him?"

"Used to run the place," Jack put in. "Killed himself."

"That's right. Killed himself right there in his study — I think the Loftuses use it for an office now. And there's a lot more to that story than most people know, too. He was a collector, of sorts. Anything to do with murder." He grimaced horribly. "Weapons, memorabilia of actual crimes, death masks..." He ran a hand through his hair, making it stand up in excited points.

"Nice guy," Skye murmured.

"You think maybe this sword stick is from that collection?" Jack asked.

"Could be. Maybe one of the guards stole it and then lost his nerve and hid it." As he spoke, Ike turned the cane over in his fingers, squinted at the hawk's head, and sighted along the length of the shaft. "The Victorians loved their secrets. Things like this often had more than one surprise... Better be careful... Zowie!"

The brass cap over the foot of the cane came off in his hand. Nestled inside it was something small that gleamed with the soft yellow sheen of gold.

Ike sank onto a rickety wooden chair behind the counter, breathing heavily. His red hair stood out like fire around a paper-white face. Skye started forward, but he waved her away.

"It's nothing. I got... a bit over-excited. That's all." After a moment he had his breath back. He grinned at them. "Not to worry! Just a touch of angina, nothing serious."

Jack wondered if it would be safe to ask about what he'd found. Before he could say anything, Ike opened his hand and tipped the golden object onto the glass-topped counter. "Pull that lamp over, will you?"

Nora hurried to move a battered goose-necked lamp so it shone down on their find. Ike rattled about in a drawer and brought out a

83

large magnifying glass. They all bent close.

"It's a ring," Skye said excitedly.

"Well, yes and no. Not a finger ring, I'd say." Ike handed the glass to Jack. He focused it and whistled softly. Someone had fashioned two tiny snakes of gold, complete with miniscule scales and eyes, and twisted them around each other so they formed a ring no bigger than a thumbnail.

"It's too small to go on anyone's finger." Jack passed the glass to Skye. "So what was it for?"

"And what was it doing in the stick?" Nora demanded.

Ike rubbed his head. "If we could find out what it was for, that might explain what it was doing there. My best guess is, it's some sort of ritual object."

"Ritual?" Nora looked puzzled. "You mean, like in church?"

"Probably not church. I suspect it's pre-Christian."

"Cool!" Skye's eyes lit up.

Ike sat down again. "And in such amazing condition! This — this could be the find of my life!"

Jack felt winded. "But if it's that old, it must be incredibly valuable!"

"If I'm right, yes." Ike looked around at them. "Which raises the question of who it belongs to. Even if the stick was Garvey's, who knows where he got the ring, and how?"

Nora suddenly closed her hand over the golden object. "I think we'd better leave now."

"Wait!" Ike jumped from his chair. Nora was backing away, clutching the ring as if she thought he might snatch it from her. "Don't you see, we need expert advice! I know a man at the Royal Ontario Museum in Toronto—"

"We can't let it go!"

"All right." He held up his hands soothingly. "Then just let me

84

take some photos. Please? I'll do my best to find out about this thing, I swear."

"Well... I guess photos wouldn't hurt. Thanks for helping," she added awkwardly.

Ike dashed into a back room and came back with a camera — not an antique, Jack noted, but a new-model Nikon. He spread a dull green cloth on the glass, placed the ring and the sword stick close together, with a yardstick set beside them to show size, and took shots of them from every angle.

"I'll head down to Toronto right away!" He waved the camera exultantly. "This is the most exciting thing that's happened to me in years!"

Skye turned toward the door, then back again. "I don't suppose you were here twenty years ago, were you, Ike?"

"Sure was. Born and bred in little old Serenity."

"Do you remember anything about what happened on the island back then? I mean, when those three kids were killed?"

"You bet I do." His face grew still. He set the camera down and sank onto the chair again. "Nobody talked of anything else for months. Three kids dead, same day, same place. And what a place! That island always had a bad name." He looked tired and ill.

"We shouldn't bother you," Nora began, but Skye persisted. "Did you know them?"

"I knew Ursula. She used to come in with her dad, often. I was in my mid-teens. Back then, my grandfather ran this store and I helped out. She was a sweet kid." He gazed at nothing for a moment, then smiled. "I was a little stuck on her. Like everybody else."

"Everybody but one person, I guess," Skye said. "What about the boys? Were they both students?"

"One was." Ike got up and moved toward the door ahead of them. "Graham Newbury, the boy who hanged himself, he was a student.

The other boy, the one who drowned, he wasn't. He was the gardener's son. Adam Shade."

Chapter 15

Life-in-Death

WITH SHAKING FINGERS, Nora slipped the snake ring into the brass cap and fitted the cap back onto the foot of the cane. Then she carefully wrapped the stick in the T-shirt again.

A moment later the three of them were standing on the porch outside the shop door. Behind the window, the OPEN sign swung around to the side that said CLOSED. Ike Frey wasted no time.

"He said... he said Adam Shade was the one who drowned." She looked from Skye to Jack. She felt as if she'd been dunked in ice water.

Jack gaped at her, then his eyes flashed with understanding. "Then of course it wasn't Adam you saw!"

"But Hedda said..."

"She said who was in that picture. Her son Adam. But your underwater lurker never told you his name, did he?"

"Well, no." Relief glimmered in her brain.

"They couldn't possibly be the same person!"

"I guess not. But then who is he?"

"Someone who happens to look like Adam. A cousin, maybe. Hedda was raised on the island. Maybe there were relatives who lived near here. Besides, how well did you ever see him?"

She remembered the darkness inside the prison and the wavering green light under the water. "Not very well, actually."

"There, see what I mean?" Jack nodded triumphantly. "If you saw him in a good light I bet he'd look nothing like Adam."

By this time the ice in her brain and body had melted. She was back in the land of the living. She caught his hand briefly in gratitude. He flushed under his tan and had no snappy comment, for once.

They headed along the village street, dodging the drops of water falling from the overhanging maples and jumping over puddles in the broken pavement.

"Still," said Skye, holding the hem of her skirt away from the wet ground, "There are a lot of things you can't explain away, Jack. Like the stick in Nora's dream turning out to actually exist."

"I never said I could explain everything. About the stick," he added, "Ike's right — we've got a problem. It doesn't belong to us."

Nora remembered her dream. "*He* says it's his."

"He?" Jack shot her a look. "Your lurker? When did he say that?"

She shrugged.

"Well, can he prove it? If it belonged to Garvey, then it's Hedda's now. And that little gold snake thing too, probably."

"Let's wait till Ike finds out more about it," she said. "I've got the funniest feeling. I don't think we should let it out of our hands."

"If Ike's right," Skye said, "that gold ring may be worth a fortune!"

"Then it should be in a museum, behind glass," Nora said. "Where people can't touch it."

THEY GOT BACK to the island at ten minutes before noon, with just enough time to go and wash up before lunch. On impulse (and a touch of paranoia, Nora admitted to herself) she let Skye go in alone. "Be up in a sec!" she called, then trotted along the north side of the house to the patch of garden border where she'd uprooted the invading creeper yesterday.

Reaching the spot, she stopped and stared. An icy wind blew down her back.

"What is it?" Jack had followed her.

"Take a look." She pointed a trembling finger. "And don't tell me that's natural!"

It wasn't obvious at first glance. The vine, or vines, had not only grown again, they had twined in among the ivy, using the other plant as a trellis and hiding place. The fine, feathery leaves were almost unnoticeable until you looked for them, and then they were everywhere. The flowers eyed her from all over the wall and winked down at her from high overhead. How high? She craned her neck.

"I think... they're almost at my window."

Jack gazed up, open-mouthed. "That's incredible! I've never heard of a plant growing that fast!" He looked at her. "Going to pull it out again?"

"What's the use? It'll just grow back. But I *am* going to close my window."

"Well, hard as it may be to believe, it's not really out to get you!" He made a clutching motion with his fingers.

This time he didn't make her smile. *Out to get me.* The cold wind was turning her spine to ice.

Jack laughed. "Come on, it's just a plant! It can't harm you!" He broke off one of the tiny blue flowers. "Look, I'll prove it to you."

"Jack, no!"

Before she could snatch it from his hand, he popped it into his mouth. He chewed, made a face, and swallowed. "Ew. Not exactly sugared violets."

Nora stared at him in horror. "You're crazy!"

"Well, maybe, but I'm not dead yet, am I?"

AFTER SOME THOUGHT, Nora decided the safest place to hide the cane and its secrets was inside one of her dresses in the closet: the plaid seersucker. She spent five minutes carefully tying the hawk's head to the zipper pull with string, and making sure it wasn't visible above the neckline.

Nobody would discover it by accident. They'd have to go looking for it, deliberately, right in that spot.

It suddenly struck her that what she was doing was completely irrational. They should have let Ike keep the thing and show it to his expert. What harm could there be in that?

And yet she felt in her bones that it ought to be kept safe, away from people. Or was it the other way around?

BETH WAS PLEASED when the four of them, Nora, Jack, Skye and Bruce, came to her in a group and asked to visit Cuthbert. After dinner they travelled with her in the pickup to Parry Sound, Skye in the cab beside Beth and the other three bumping and jostling in the box behind.

Cuthbert was well enough to spend an hour with his wife, and to joke with the rest of them for a few minutes. "He'll be home in two days," Beth said cheerfully, when they left. "He won't be very mobile, but we'll manage."

It was dark when the truck rattled across the bridge again. As they passed the tangle of climbing roses at the inner end and turned left onto the gravelled road, Nora, facing backwards in the box, saw a man-shaped shadow separate from the blackness of the tangle and raise a hand, beckoning.

Ten minutes later she left Skye, Jack and Bruce with the other students who were reading or texting or playing ping pong or watching TV in the common room. Nobody seemed to notice when she slipped from the room and let herself out the front door.

The moon stood overhead, still nearly full. It whitened the road under her feet. To her right, the waves glittered as they nibbled at the silver-lit beach. To her left, the forest was inky and unfathomable.

90

Will he still be there? she wondered as she ran. Her mouth was dry, her heart hammering. She ran faster, to keep herself from forming thoughts. But the thoughts still came. *He terrifies me. Why am I doing this? If I didn't go, I'd always wonder what I'd missed. I must be insane!*

She came pelting around the bend, and then stopped short in a scatter of gravel, breathless. He was leaning against the end post of the bridge, below the arch of climbing roses, gazing down into the rushing water of the channel. As she walked toward him he turned and looked at her. Moonlight traced the line of his cheekbones and brow. It was a face you might have seen on an old coin, some ancient king or god.

She stood still and they looked at each other. After a tense moment she blurted, "Will I ever see you by daylight?"

He laughed, breaking the spell. The laugh made him younger, more ordinary, though still far more beautiful than any boy had a right to be.

"With your help, Nora, I'll soon be able to do anything I want."

It was the first time she'd actually heard his voice: in her ears, not just in her head. An unexpectedly soft voice, yet deep, like dark brown velvet, warm on her skin.

"What do you mean, with my help? Do what? Who— who are you?"

His eyebrows quirked. "You already know. My name is in your head, I can read it there."

She backed away, too chilled to speak. "You can't be."

"But I am!" He laughed again, and the night wind blew a strand of dark hair into his eyes. He flicked it away. She saw now that his eyes were the only thing that showed any colour in the silvering moonlight. They shone a warm russet. She'd never seen eyes that colour before, almost red. Except... Hedda.

"Don't be afraid," he said softly. "I need your help."

"But Adam's d-dead." She took another step back, then another.

"It's not that simple." He didn't try to follow, just stood still, watching, as she backed farther away. It seemed to her that lines of despair etched into his face as she retreated.

She stopped. Bone-shaking fear fought with incredulity, disbelief with fascination. *Am I really having this conversation or am I dreaming again?*

"Dead is dead," she managed.

"No. There's life and there's death. And then there's life-in-death." The lines smoothed from his face as he watched her. "I'm a prisoner, Nora. I'm chained here where I don't belong." He tilted his head back at the bridge. "I can't even cross that water."

"What do you mean, chained? How?"

"That talisman you found, the twined snakes, that's my chain. Ursula and I buried it in the garden, to keep it safe. It was meant to bind us together always. But then he stole her from me." His eyes suddenly glowed, more red than russet.

She backed away again, and he raised his head. "Don't go!"

"Who do you mean? Who stole her?"

"Graham, of course. He killed her when he found out she loved me. He was crazy with jealousy." The glow in his eyes died. "I lost Ursula, my life, everything. And because of the talisman, I'm bound here forever. Forever."

Forever... The word echoed in Nora's mind, bringing such loneliness and weariness that she let out a cry. That he should be condemned to an eternity of such misery.... It was unbearable.

"You can help, Nora."

"I can? How?"

He let out a long sigh, as if until this very moment he'd feared she would refuse. "There's a spring on the island. Do you know it?"

She nodded, keeping her eyes on his.

"Take the talisman and drown it. Drown it deep in the flowing water. Then I'll be free."

"Is that all?"

"Seems too easy, doesn't it?" He smiled. "But yes, that's all."

She stood shivering, clenching and unclenching her hands. Torn between fear and pity. It seemed easy, yes, but another voice was nagging at her, trying to tell her something. Too many voices, all talking across each other. Her hands clutched at her head, tried to corral her milling thoughts.

He watched, his smile gone. His eyes were dark and sad. "Nora," he whispered. "Please don't leave me like this."

A rush of pity swept away fear. She reached out a hand. His eyes sprang to life again, and his hand rose to meet hers. At that a half-buried memory cropped up, of the one time she'd touched his hand, yesterday under the water. When his eyes had held her there. When she might have drowned again. She hesitated, and in that moment voices behind her broke the quiet.

"There she is! I told you I saw her going this way!" Skye's voice.

Nora looked over her shoulder and saw Skye and Jack jogging along the road toward her. When she looked back at Adam, he was gone.

Chapter 16

Drowning the Ring

"WAIT! Come back!"

Jack panted to a halt at her side. "Who was that?"

"You mean you saw him?"

"Saw who?" Skye demanded.

"I saw him, all right." Jack said in a flat voice. "Took off like a scalded cat. Was that your lurker?"

Nora closed her eyes briefly. Until this moment she hadn't been one hundred per cent certain Adam was real. Or that she'd actually stood there talking with him under the moon. Now she was sure. "Yes, that was Adam."

Skye drew her breath in. Jack made an incredulous noise. "Nora, are you crazy? Meeting this guy out here alone?"

"But it's Adam!"

"Did he say so? Then he's lying! Adam's dead!"

"But..." She looked back at the bridge.

Skye took her firmly by the arm and turned her back toward the school. "Come on, you're shivering! Let's go back, we'll get some hot chocolate and talk this over. Mr. Trust-No-One can come along or not, whatever he likes."

"Look," Jack said from Nora's other side, "you don't really think you've been talking to a ghost, do you? Of course not! So he has to be lying, trying to con you. Or, worse, he's off his onion. Those are the only two choices."

"But he knew about the talisman!" She pulled free of Skye's grip.

"The snake ring? A talisman? Is that what he called it?" Skye asked eagerly.

"Yes. But the point is," Nora looked at Jack, "how could he know about that thing if he wasn't Adam?"

He scowled. "He's been following us and spying on us, that's how. Nora, this is getting serious. This creep could be dangerous!"

They walked on in uncomfortable silence, until they'd rounded the bend and the school building loomed up ahead of them, studded with squares of golden light.

"There's something else that's been bothering me." Nora stopped and looked at both their faces. "Why did he choose me? Why not anybody else? Why me?"

Jack opened his mouth, but Skye cut him off. "I've been wondering that too. And now it occurs to me." She pointed a silver-nailed finger at Nora. "You said you were sick last year. How sick?"

Nora looked at the bay, a sparkling expanse beyond the strip of moonlit beach. Deliberately she walked down to the water. Small waves broke in a shining strip and ran up to wet her toes.

It might as well come out now. She turned and faced them. Skye looked expectant, Jack worried.

"Remember I said I had appendicitis? That was last September. I was swimming at a beach in the Ottawa River. When the attack hit me I nearly drowned." Nora closed her eyes, then quickly opened them again. It was too easy to relive those moments of pain and panic, and the swallowing darkness that had been the worst of all.

"Actually, I did drown. I was under water for three minutes. When they pulled me out, my heart wasn't beating. They had to restart it."

Skye clapped her hands. "That's it, then! Near-death experiences often change people. It brought you closer to the unseen."

"You think? Well, I don't want to be closer to the unseen, thanks

95

very much." Nora shuddered. Then squared her shoulders. Best to finish what she'd started.

"There's something else you should know. After the appendicitis and the drowning, I caught pneumonia and then bronchitis. I spent a lot of time cooped up at home. While I was sick, I... well... I saw things that... that weren't there. Not dreams: these things happened when I was awake." She studied their faces. Jack's worried expression hadn't changed.

Skye looked interested. "Really? What did you see?"

"Strange people walking through the walls of my room. A view of a river where our garden was supposed to be. Once, a black dog jumped onto the bed and growled at me. Things like that."

"Sweet! And did anything like that ever happen to you before you drowned?"

"No. Never."

"So being dead, or nearly, made you more open to the influence of the other world. This is so cool!" Skye did a little dance on the spot.

"Cool? Not so much." Nora kept her eyes on Jack's face. "I overheard my mother talking to the doctor about my 'stories.' She was worried the drowning might have caused brain damage."

"So of course you worried too." Jack held out a hand. "And you've been worrying ever since, right? That's too long. Come on, that hot chocolate sounds good."

After a moment she took his hand and they walked together up the beach toward the school, with Skye picking her way daintily in front. Nora felt airy-headed with relief. She knew then how afraid she'd been. Afraid that he would think she was crazy, if she told him the dreadful truth about herself. Afraid his open face would close, the smile in his eyes would blink out.

"You act as if everybody and his brother has hallucinations," she

96

said as they walked, swinging hands.

"Well, you were sick. No big deal. And I can see," he added, "why you were so happy when that gate in the prison yard turned out to be an actual gate."

"Right." She laughed. "And that's why I'd rather Adam was an actual ghost instead of just a figment of my crazed imagination."

"Isn't 'actual ghost' a contradiction?"

"I have an open mind about it. Ghosts could be something real that we haven't managed to explain yet. Don't you think?"

He wagged his head back and forth, considering. "Well, okay, maybe it's just barely possible that some weird things are real. The gate in the wall, the stick in the dream. But," he swung her hand again for emphasis, "don't let's get carried away! I'm still willing to bet this Adam is ordinary flesh and blood. Which makes him a lot more dangerous, in my opinion, than any ghost."

THE ROOM was silent except for Skye's even breathing, and dark except for a bar of moonlight printed across the floor. Nora pushed back the quilt, stood up and walked silently to the closet.

She needed no light to find the sword stick hanging inside the dress. Careful not to let the hangers clink, she felt up inside the dress, found the shaft, slid the brass cap off the end and dropped the talisman into her hand.

Replacing the brass cap, she closed the closet door without a sound and walked out of the room. Skye hadn't stirred. Moments later Nora was downstairs, gliding across the lobby's black and white floor. The lock on the front door clicked over quietly. The heavy door swung open at her push.

The night air was damp and cool, and she wore only a pair of thin cotton pyjamas, but she felt no chill. In the moonlight her way was clear. Swift as thought she left the house and its gardens and greenhouse behind. The hill rose before her, black against the starry sky. Her bare feet skimmed up the timber steps, and then the forest folded her in.

In and out of flickering patches of moonlight and shadow she flitted, never a stumble, never a slide. Climbing now. Reaching for rocks and roots with her left hand. Even with her right hand clenched around the snake ring, she never lost her footing. At the top of the knoll the trees stood back in a circle, hollowing out a clearing. Moonlight flooded in and spotlit the spring in its granite basin.

The pool was small, no more than two feet across. Its surface was black, glassy except for a wrinkle at the centre that marked where the current surged up from below. It sparkled like cut glass where it spilled over a rocky lip and gurgled away southward toward the bay.

Nora didn't hesitate. She stood on the stony brink, arms at her sides, talisman safe in her right fist. One outward step, and her body became a spear slicing straight down.

Bubbles streamed from her mouth as she sank. Her arms rose. She held up the talisman and saw the wavering disk of the moon inside its circle. Power boiled away from it like black smoke into the scouring stream.

Only then did she understand, for one moment, what she had done. Numbness became cold, then pain. Then came a crushing darkness, blotting out the moon and sucking her down.

Chapter 17

The Hangman

"NORA. NORA!" Fingers dug into her arm, a voice shouted in her ear. "Nora!"

"What... Where... Dr. Beth?"

"You were sleepwalking. Don't be frightened, you're not far from the school. You'll be fine."

They were standing beside the spring. Nora was shaking with cold. Her feet felt gritty and sore. But her pyjamas — she touched them — were dry. Her right hand hurt and she uncurled it. She had been clutching the talisman so tightly that it was cutting into her palm. She slipped it into her left hand and made a loose fist.

Beth, who was fully dressed, shone her flashlight down the knoll toward the deer track. "Let's get you back to the house, you're chilled. Hold my arm — that's it. There we go."

As they picked their way along the forest path and down the hill, Beth talked soothingly. "Have you sleepwalked before? No? Then it may be just a fluke. Stress can cause sleep disturbances of that kind. Are you feeling unusually stressed these days, Nora?"

"Well, maybe a little." *Understatement of the year!*

"I thought that might be it. Try to get extra rest tomorrow. Good thing I was up late marking problem papers and saw you pass my window. You'd have had a very rude awakening if you'd taken one more step!"

"NORA, YOU COULD have drowned!" Jack dropped his fork, scattering bits of scrambled egg over the table. "That water's cold enough to paralyze you in seconds. And who knows how deep it is?"

The refectory bustled around them. Students carried filled plates from the kitchen hatch, cutlery clinked, conversation buzzed. Warm morning air drifted in through tall windows, coffee cups steamed, savoury smells floated on the breeze. It was all reassuringly normal. So normal that Nora's story of sleepwalking at midnight sounded bizarre, hard even for her to believe.

"Adam must not have realized the danger." Skye finished a piece of toast and licked her buttery fingers. "I mean, he only wanted her to drown the talisman. He couldn't have wanted her to drown herself!"

"You think Adam made this happen?" Jack thumped the table with his fist. "Come on! Let's get our feet back on the ground, okay? You're still assuming he's got some special—"

"Keep your voice down!" Skye tilted her head at the next table over, where a younger boy and girl were staring at them with open interest. She bent across the table and lowered her voice. "All right, how about this? Nora doesn't know anything about the occult. I mean, barring her own experiences. How could she have known about the power of spring water? And if she didn't know, she couldn't dream about it, right? Not unless Adam put that idea into her head!"

Nora wrapped chilled fingers around her coffee cup. "I haven't the faintest notion what you're talking about."

"You see?" Skye nodded smugly. "For your information, both of you, a flowing spring is one of the most powerful cleansing magics there is." Jack let out a hoot and took breath to speak. Skye waved him down. "No, just listen for once, okay? Psychic influences can't match the power of flowing water. This one even flows in the right direction — south. What Adam was telling Nora to do was take that talisman and wash away whatever power it has. To neutralize it."

"But — even if I buy this," Jack said, "and I'm a long way from buying, why would he want it neutralized?"

Nora pushed away her half-empty plate. "Because it's keeping him here where he doesn't belong." They both looked at her. Skye's eyebrows rose, Jack's eyes narrowed. Briefly, she passed on what Adam had told her last night.

"Oh, Nora." Skye's eyelashes were damp. "That's so incredibly sad! Lost his love, lost his life, and still bound here by a love charm."

"That's incredible crap." Jack dug into his scrambled eggs.

Skye ignored him. "You're going to do it, of course. You're going to set him free. Right? I'll help, of course. It should be after sunset, I think, and we'll have to be careful to keep absolute silence on the way: that's important. We could..."

"Wait." Nora held up both hands. "I'll do it, but not until we've heard from Ike."

Jack blew out a breath of relief. "Good thinking."

"And until then, Jack, I want you to keep the thing."

"Me? Why me?" He sat back warily.

"Because I think it will be safer with you. Suppose I walk in my sleep again? Or, or start doing something else I have no control over? I'll go get it right now, and you can hide it, and the stick too. I don't want to know where it is." She stood up, and for a moment leaned against the table, eyes closed.

"You okay?" Jack's hand reached for her arm, hovered, fell.

Her eyes blinked open and she smiled at him. "I'm just so tired. My thoughts are all fuzzy. Funny... when I've had anything to do with Adam, it's hard for me to think straight."

"Well, if he's the one who sent you sleepwalking, he was using you," Jack said fiercely. "I don't care if he's ghost or flesh and blood — whatever he is, he's a jerk and I don't trust him an inch!"

THAT THOUGHT was on his mind as he headed toward the class-room wing twenty minutes later. He was early: first class wouldn't start for another fifteen minutes, but there was something he wanted to do. And should have done long before this, he thought.

The Loftuses' office door was half open when he reached it. He knocked on the jamb and stepped inside. "Dr. Beth?" She wasn't there, but her desk was covered with papers and her computer was turned on, so obviously she'd just stepped out.

Jack waited, hands in pockets, rocking back and forth on his heels. It was a nice room, in a teacherish kind of way. Then he re-membered what Ike had said yesterday. This was where Erwin Gar-vey, the last, disgraced governor of the jail, had blown his brains out fifty years ago. His spine prickled.

The thought came: if the house had ghosts, this room would be the place for them.

Except he didn't believe in ghosts. At least, he was almost com-pletely sure he didn't.

In the last few days, though, he'd had to open his eyes to a lot of strangeness. Sealed gates that unsealed themselves, flowers that grew a mile a minute, love/hate charms that might or might not work, dowsing that actually did. And it all centred around Nora, he thought uneasily.

He squared his shoulders and turned on the spot, searching, in-specting. The old hardwood floor was partly covered by a red-and-gold carpet with a complicated mazelike design all over it, tempting the eye to follow and see if the maze led anywhere. The walls were mostly bookshelves, some behind glass, except where the window opened up a big square of brightness. There was a comfy-looking small sofa in one corner under a reading lamp.

No, it was still a nice room. If Garvey had left any bad vibes here, the Loftuses' good vibes had long ago scoured them out.

102

Beth still wasn't back. He shifted from foot to foot for another minute. Then, spotting a framed photograph on the desk with its back toward him, he circled around to see it.

He realized at once who this must be. A girl of about 16, pretty, with a rounded face and long gold-blond hair. But it was the eyes that made the face special. He picked up the picture to get a better look. If the reproduction was true, she had eyes of an amazing colour, an intense summer-sky blue. A clear, pure blue that seemed to harbour no secrets or lies.

Beth walked in the door. He jumped, feeling guilty, and set the picture down. A shadow passed over her face. She didn't smile. "Something I can do for you, Jack?"

"I — um, yes." He cleared his throat. "I thought I should tell you about this guy who's been hanging around the island."

Her eyes sharpened. "What guy?"

"I don't know, that's the problem. He's maybe seventeen, maybe eighteen, but he's not one of the students. I've seen him a couple of times. I think he might be sneaking around to bother the girls."

"Any idea who it might be?"

"Well, he looks..." Quick thought: can't mention the name Adam Shade, not to her. "Um, not like anybody I know."

"All right, Jack, thanks for telling me. I'll ask the staff to keep an eye out, and I'll mention this to the officers at our local O.P.P. detachment. It wouldn't be the first time some village boy has made a nuisance of himself."

JACK MEANT TO HEAD straight on to the classroom wing then, but he had another (he looked at his watch), oh, eight minutes. Still one more useful thing he could do before buckling down to a fun morning of remedial math. Sitting in the refectory at breakfast, watching disembodied hands pass plates of food through the serving hatch, he'd made a mental note.

That cook Skye had mentioned — Mrs. Duggan, was it? — who'd been here when the school opened all those years ago. Obvious person to tackle. She must know just about everything that happened here.

He backtracked to the refectory, deserted now, the hatch shut. A two-way swing door in the far wall led to the built-on kitchen. He pushed open the door and poked his head in. The only person in the room was a thin woman in her mid-thirties wearing a long white apron over khaki shorts and T-shirt, with a net enclosing a bundle of brown braids. She was rolling out dough on a marble-topped counter.

She frowned when she saw him. "If you're looking for breakfast, you're out of luck. Try getting up on time after this."

"I've had breakfast, thanks." He came in and let the door swing closed behind him. The kitchen was a big room, hot despite the high ceiling and wide-open windows, its tile floor islanded with tables and counters covered with dishes and cooking tools. From somewhere nearby, Jack guessed the next room, came the rattle of crockery, the hum of a dishwasher and the warble of an off-key soprano. He wondered if that was the cook, and if this woman rolling dough was Zoe.

He strolled forward, hands in pockets, offering his most winning smile. "Is Mrs. Duggan around?"

"I'm Mrs. Duggan." The rolling pin kept rolling.

"Oh!" He felt foolish. Another stereotype down the drain. He'd been expecting someone fat and cheerful and grandmotherly. "Then, hey, thanks for breakfast!" He restored the smile. "But actually I wondered if you could tell me something about somebody."

"Depends. Who and what?"

"Mrs. Shade. Does she have any relatives living near here?" Seeing her eyes narrow, he quickly added, "I only ask because I think I may have seen somebody who's related to her. There's a guy been

104

hanging around the island, and I want to know who he is."

"Why don't you ask Hedda?"

He shrugged, hands still in pockets. "She's... well... not very askable."

She grinned, showing white teeth. "Huh, yeah. Hmm..." She considered, meanwhile slicing the pastry into squares. "I guess it can do no harm to answer your question, especially as the answer is No." She dropped ladlefuls of chopped apple onto the squares of pastry.

"But she grew up here."

"Yeah, but the Garveys weren't local and didn't mix. Came from Toronto — one of those old-money WASP families. And so far as I know Hedda has no friends around here either. That's not really her fault. Being Garvey's daughter can't have been easy."

Jack leaned against the marble slab and watched as she sprinkled the chopped apples with flour and sugar and cinnamon. He was starting to feel hungry again. "Do people still remember him?"

"Darn right they do! Some in the village used to be prisoners in that jail. Some used to be guards. My own grandfather was a guard. He never said much, just that there would've been fewer 'accidental' deaths among the prisoners if the governor had been anybody else but Garvey. He said the guards had a nickname for him." She paused in the middle of folding up a pastry, and thought back, then nodded. "They called him the Hangman."

Jack whistled softly. What a father to have. No wonder Hedda was all sour and twisted.

"This guy you mentioned." The cook was folding and pinching another pastry pocket. "Why'd you think he might be related to Hedda?"

"Because he looks just like Adam Shade. He—"

Her fingers clenched and the pastry split, spilling bits of apple onto the marble slab. "Now see what you made me do!"

105

"You know something about him, don't you?" Jack straightened up. "You know what happened?"

"I can't stand here yakking, I have too much work to do. Out you go!"

Her tone and face left no room for argument. "Well, thanks anyway." He turned and headed for the door.

"Hey!"

He spun around.

"What's your name?"

"Jack."

"Melinda." She jerked a floury thumb at herself. "Jack, no offense, but some things are better left buried. Safer that way. Don't get too curious, eh?"

Chapter 18
Predator

THEY SPENT A QUIET morning and afternoon at their books and computers, making up for time lost the day before. Later they swam, diving off the pier and stroking through the cool water to the swim platform.

After watching from the shore for half an hour, Nora grimly waded into the water and splashed back and forth in the shallows. With Jack there to call encouragement, for a few minutes she forgot her fears and enjoyed herself. But she was still careful to keep her head above the surface.

As they were walking up toward the school in the afterglow of sunset, swinging their towels, a phone rang inside the building. Beth stepped out the side door and waved at them. It was for Nora.

"What's wrong? Is it my mom?"

"Don't look so worried!" Beth smiled. "No, it's Ike Frey. Something you asked him to look into, he says."

"Oh, good!" Nora set off at a run, the other two pelting behind her. She took the phone call in the common room with Skye at one elbow and Jack at the other, both straining to hear.

"We've got to meet." Ike's voice bounced excitedly over the line. "Have I got things to tell you!"

"Did you find out something about it?"

"Wait'll you hear! I spent half of yesterday and half of today finding out about it. Just got back from Toronto — flew to Parry Sound, drove home — worn out!"

"Oh my gosh." She thought of his heart condition. "You'd better rest. We can meet tomorrow."

"No, this can't wait. Nora, that talisman is a unique piece, absolutely wonderful!" He laughed, then took a ragged breath. "Also horrible, if you believe half the stuff I was told."

"Do you want us to come to the village, then?"

"No, I'll drive to the island. Fifteen minutes! I'll leave the car on the far side and meet you on your side of the bridge." The phone clicked off.

"Fifteen minutes?" Skye demanded, when she heard the message. "That doesn't even give us time to change!"

"It's plenty of time," Nora said firmly. She ran up the stairs, taking them by twos. Something in Ike's excitement had set a prickling in her bones.

Less than ten minutes later, after a quick change into shorts and T-shirt and a pair of old sneakers, she was waiting at the bottom of the stairs. Jack ran down to join her, pulling a shirt on over his head as he came and nearly missing a step. He caught the handrail and jumped the last two.

"Skye late?"

"Of course, and I'm afraid Ike will be early."

"That shouldn't be a problem. He'll wait, if he's so excited about this thing."

"It's not that. It's... I can't explain. I feel something's going to happen."

"Happen? What?"

"I don't know!" She danced from foot to foot, glanced impatiently up the stairwell, then made a decision. "Come on!"

She wrestled the front door open and was out and running. Suddenly every moment was precious. Jack came pounding after her, too breathless or too smart to ask questions.

Ten minutes had been long enough to drain most of the gold from the sky. Close to the water, with its reflected light, you could still see your way, but soon it would be too dark to run without stumbling. She put her head down and sprinted.

As they ran, she listened for the grumble of a car engine. But when the sound came, faintly above the thud and crunch of their feet on the gravel road, it was not an engine. It was a thin human sound.

Nora caught Jack's arm and they stood still, panting, straining their ears. There was nothing to hear now. A shush of waves on hard sand, the distant cry of a nighthawk: that was all. The empty road curved ahead of them along the beach. The bridge was out of sight beyond the next bend.

Jack shifted his feet. "Maybe this was a bad idea." He glanced up the slope toward the woods, already thick with darkness.

He could be up there, Nora thought. Adam. He could be standing a few feet back from the edge of the woods, invisible in blackness, watching.

Then the sound came again. No mistake this time: it was a cry for help, suddenly cut off.

"Get back to the house!" Jack started running.

She didn't bother to answer. In two strides she caught up to him and they sprinted down the road side by side.

Nora spotted it first, just as they rounded the last bend before the bridge. Somebody was struggling at the edge of the shore, splashing half in and half out of the water. "Ike!" she yelled. He stopped splashing. There was something not right about his shape. It looked as if more than one person crouched there.

As she slid down the bank toward him, the shape broke apart. A solid shadow rose above Ike's shoulder and looked at her, hostile and wary, like a wild animal disturbed at its feeding. But the shape of the shadow was human, and the feral glow of the eyes was not opalescent green but burning red.

Nora froze. As she stared, Jack pushed past her and grabbed at the limp body in the shallows. The shadowy shape slid away into the thickening night.

Chapter 19

The Talisman

WITH NORA'S HELP, Jack pulled Ike out of the water and laid him down on the sparse grass at the top of the bank, with his head lower than his feet.

"On his side, so he won't choke," Nora said. They rolled him over, and a little water trickled out of his mouth.

"What is it? What's happened?" Skye came running along the road and dropped down on the grass beside them.

"I don't know!" Jack snapped. "Get Beth, phone for an ambulance — hurry!" Skye was off again in a flurry of skirts.

"Is he..." Nora couldn't finish.

"No, he's breathing."

But even in the twilight she could see Ike's face was slack and colourless. "I should have told him not to come!"

"How could you have stopped him?" Jack had two fingers on the pulse at the side of Ike's neck. "This doesn't feel good," he muttered. "It must have been a heart attack. All the excitement. He must have been standing at the top of the bank when he fell."

"Heart attack? But didn't you see..."

"Yes. I saw."

Ike's lips moved. "Papers." Nora had to lean close to make out the sound. "Pocket."

Jack slipped his hand into the nearest pocket in Ike's windbreaker. He brought out a roll of half-soaked pages. "Got them!" He stuffed them into the back pocket of his shorts.

"Promise... read..."

"We will, I promise," Jack said, too loud, too cheerful. "Don't talk any more, just take it easy. You'll be fine! Help will be here any minute."

"The talisman. You... still... have...." Ike's voice was all breath now. He struggled to get up on one elbow. Jack pressed him back down. Behind them on the road came the pounding of many pairs of feet.

"Don't worry, we've got it hidden."

Ike's hand clutched at Nora's. "Maybe more... in this... than... I thought. Be... care..."

"Ike, who was that with you?"

His lips moved, then stilled. His head lolled back on the grass. His eyes reflected the moon.

"Ike!"

Jack started blowing air into Ike's mouth. A moment later Beth arrived, with Skye scurrying behind her and Hedda thumping along in the rear.

"The paramedics are on their way." Beth knelt beside Jack. She made a sound of distress.

Minutes passed: too many, Nora knew, but she also knew it was already too late. Beth and Jack took turns working over Ike, filling and emptying his lungs, pumping on his heart.

Nora stood back and watched, fists clenched at her sides, trying not to think. But thoughts wormed through her defences. *That red-eyed thing I saw with Ike, that was Adam. The real Adam. That monster: I talked to it, I touched its hand. I pitied it, for God's sake!*

When they caught the distant wail of an ambulance siren, everyone breathed a sigh of relief. Not that it would do Ike any good, Nora thought miserably.

She made herself look again at his empty face. He'd been so

alive, with his flaming hair and his laughing eyes, his enthusiasm. How he'd danced around the shop! All that gone now. She shivered.

When she looked up, Hedda was gazing at her across Ike's body. No, wait. She wasn't gazing at Nora: she was looking over Nora's shoulder, past her, and her face was stiff with disbelief and... was that wonder? Her eyes lit with something that Nora would have sworn was joy.

But when she turned around to look, nothing was there but the empty road.

THEY WERE SITTING midway up the curving staircase, waiting for Beth to come back, although she had told them not to wait up. Nora sat lower down, Jack a couple of steps above her, Skye above him.

The big house drowsed around them. The common room had emptied. The other students, including Bruce, were in their rooms, sleeping or studying. Except for the chandelier that glittered almost level with their eyes, all nearby lights were out. They sat in a pool of radiance hedged by darkness.

It had taken them ten minutes to separate Ike's papers. The damp pages had kept their ink, but they were soft, and tore easily. They laid them out on the edges of the stairs next to the railing: photocopies of articles from academic journals, pictures of serpent rings from different cultures, and "Notes from my Conversation with Dr. Yeats," in a swift, looping scrawl that had to be Ike's.

" 'Definitely Celtic,' he says. I think." Jack puzzled over Ike's handwriting, which must have been hard to read at the best of times. " 'Likely fifth century BC, similar to objects found near Rodenbach, Germany. Museum quality. Trace...'" He squinted. "Looks like 'province.' No, 'provenance,' whatever that is. And then here." He looked up. " 'Nasty piece of work,' he says."

"This article is all about love charms." Skye bent over the limp

113

sheet spread out on her palms. "But they don't sound very loving to me. Listen: 'If the goal was to dominate the object of one's affections, forcing that person to become one's lover, then the procedure was to secrete the charm within the desired one's house, preferably within the bedstead.' Then down here it says, 'The same sort of charm could, it was believed, be used to conquer an enemy. Secreted within some attractive object and presented to him as a peace-offering, assuming he were to accept the gift, the charm would work upon him like a slowly ingested poison, sapping and ultimately destroying his will.' "

"Which do you suppose Adam meant it to be?" Jack wondered. "Love charm or hate charm?"

"He said he and Ursula buried it to keep it safe, to bind them together forever," Nora said. "And then Graham killed her. Out of jealousy."

"Well, that's Adam's version of what happened." Jack thought of the girl in the photo, with her clear blue eyes. "I don't think Ursula had anything to do with it."

"So..." Nora carefully spread out the papers again. "What should we do with the talisman?"

Skye considered. "There is one thing we could do, and it would get Adam off your back."

Jack looked up. "I'm all for that. What?"

"Do what he says. Neutralize it." She spread her hands. "It's what he wants, isn't it? To be set free?"

Nora wiped damp fingers on her shorts. "Yeah, but free to do what?"

"To leave this earth." Skye said solemnly. "To finally enter the spirit world."

Jack watched hope and fear chase each other across Nora's face. He held his breath, waiting for her to say what he was thinking.

"He never said he wants to leave the world. Just this island." She met Jack's eyes. " I'm afraid to set him loose."

"Me too."

Skye fluffed her long skirts, dissatisfied. "Sounds like you two have made up your minds. Didn't he say he doesn't want to be tied here any more? He—"

Jack broke in. "Would you believe anything you heard from that thing we saw with Ike? It looked like it was feeding off him!" He saw Nora shudder.

Skye said dryly, "So you don't think, any longer, this is just some village boy."

"Nope. Can't."

"Then what are we going to do about him?" Skye tossed her hair back. "To tell the truth, folks, this is way beyond me. If he really is what we're thinking, what the heck can we do?"

"Way beyond me too," Nora said. "But we have to do something. I mean, I will. I can't just run off home and leave things like this, not after what he did to Ike. I mean, who's next? I'd feel better if I was sure the talisman is safe right now."

She propped her head on her hands. She looked white and exhausted. Jack wondered how much sleep she'd had, the last few nights.

"At least I can check on that. Won't be a minute."

He jumped up and ran up the stairs to the third floor. Pushing open the door of his room, he crossed to his dresser, quietly, so as not to wake Bruce, and pulled the middle drawer right out. He dumped a tangle of socks and underwear on the dresser top and flipped the drawer over in his hands.

Oh crap.

That morning he'd taken the talisman out of the sword stick, wrapped it in a small plastic bag and taped the bag to the bottom of

115

the drawer. But maybe he had the wrong drawer? Maybe... He shoved it back in and pulled out the drawer below. Nothing taped to its underside, either.

A cold, sick feeling crept into his stomach.

"Lost something?"

Jack looked up to see Bruce propped up on one elbow, watching him through half-open eyes.

"Why? Did you find something?"

"Nope." Bruce lay back, rolled over and began breathing evenly.

Jack checked the other drawers in his dresser. And then, deliberately, he searched Bruce's dresser, inside and out. Then he searched both closets, and all the clothes in them. Through it all Bruce lay as if asleep, but he wasn't snoring, so Jack was skeptical.

He searched the entire room, but he already knew what he would find. Nothing.

Chapter 20

Eyes Like Embers

AS JACK CAME BACK downstairs, two pairs of eyes swivelled up at him. "Bad news," he muttered.

"Oh no!" Nora closed her eyes.

He nodded. "Right. I still have the sword stick, hidden, but the talisman's gone." He described his search.

After he finished, Skye stood up and purposefully gathered the folds of her skirt in one hand. "My brother the rat! Leave him to me."

"It may be too late," Nora said. "And he may not be a rat. Maybe he was used the way I was used last night."

"You mean," Jack said, "maybe he took it in his sleep?"

"Hm, yeah, it would have to be that way." Skye plumped down again. "Bruce thinks all of this, Adam and the rest, it's a waste of time. There's no reason why he'd bother with the talisman. Unless he didn't know what he was doing."

Jack sat down on the steps above the girls and stared at his clasped hands. Skye had it right, he thought: Bruce being the unimaginative hard-head that he was, the only explanation for his out-of-character behaviour would have to be an irrational one.

"Like I said," Nora said softly, "if Bruce took the talisman, it may already be neutralized. That would change everything. Then what?"

Nobody could think of anything useful to say. A few minutes later they heard the crunch of tires and the thud of a car door. The front door swung open. Beth stepped in and stopped with her hand on the handle, running her eyes up the stairs and the faces tiered above each other. "Didn't I tell you not to wait up?"

"We wanted to," Jack said.

"Did you?" Beth closed the door, then locked it. "I hope you haven't been blaming yourselves. I've talked to Ike's family."

"Was he married?" Skye asked. "Did he have kids?"

"No." (Skye looked as relieved as Jack felt.) "He lived with some cousins. They said his heart was very frail. He knew he was living on borrowed time. Any stress at all could have killed him."

"Easy prey," Nora said under her breath, but Jack heard.

"There's some question, though, about why he was on the island." Beth's eyes moved from face to face. "Can any of you shed any light?"

"He came to see me," Nora said quickly. "I had an old ring and I took it to him to see if it was worth anything. He checked into it and he thought it was, and he wanted to tell me right away. That's why he came."

It was near the truth, Jack thought, but it left out so much, it might as well be an outright lie. Nora bit her lip, looking savage. Mad at herself.

Beth studied her. Then her face softened. "It's not your fault. Will you try to remember that?" Nora ducked her head in what might have been a nod. Beth waved them up and away. "Now off to bed, the three of you. If you have bad dreams, come and tell me."

"NORA.... NORA...." Someone was calling her name. The voice was just a thread, but it clung like spider silk, it wrapped around her, it tugged her toward a door that swung open on blackness.

She woke with a gasp, her heart pounding. Wide awake, she heard echoes fading in the corners of the room, as if the small, square space had grown caverns and tunnels in the dark hours. The darkness was deep and hollow, thick with whispers.

She sat up and listened. Nothing to hear now but the usual faint creaks of a dry old house, and the even rhythm of Skye's breathing. Just another dream, she told herself. An ordinary nightmare.

That didn't help. Instead of growing calm, she grew restless. A sense of danger crept down her spine on spidery feet. Something was coming. Something bad. The feeling grew until she couldn't sit still. She slipped from bed and crossed to the window, which was closed and latched. Whatever was coming, it had to be out there.

Moonlight winked off the panes of the greenhouse and bathed everything else in bright silver. Nobody was out there, that was easy to see. Nobody stood on the pale sweep of turf or moved in the vegetable garden.

Nothing moved at all except the cloud of blue-eyed flowers stirring around the outside of her window. Wanting a breath of fresh air she opened the window, half expecting them to claw at the screen with their wiry stems, prepared to slam the sash down.

They stayed put. Moist air sieved through them, carrying their bittersweet smell. It cleared her head with a rush, and she found herself breathing deeply. Cuthbert was right, she thought. It is a refreshing scent.

She raised the screen a hand's breadth, reached through and picked a single blossom. She held it against her cheek and simply breathed. Funny, how sometimes things made better sense by night, when you were the only one awake and the world was quiet.

These flowers, now.... They'd scared her, the weird way they grew and behaved. The way they seemed to be targeting her. And yet in the jail yard that time, when they pinned her down, hadn't they been trying to keep her from doing something?

From finding the sword stick and the talisman. Right.

"And if I'd only understood what they were trying to tell me, maybe all this wouldn't have happened." She leaned her forehead against the window frame. "Maybe Ike would still be alive."

She looked at the blue blossom in her fingers. "Or maybe not. For Pete's sake, they're just flowers!"

Skye's bed creaked. "Wha... Nora? Something wrong?"

"I don't know. I thought so but I guess it was just a bad dream."

"See anything out there?"

"No." Nora closed the window.

Skye sat up, stretched and yawned. "I'm incredibly hungry. Got anything stashed away?"

"No, sorry."

"Well, I've got to eat or I won't sleep. It's what, two? Two-thirty? Hey, I wonder if they lock the kitchen at night."

"Wait a minute, you're not going down there!"

"Why not? You just said you don't think there's anything wrong." Skye slipped out of bed and tossed a white silk robe over her lacy nightgown.

Nora rubbed her chilled arms. "I can't see anything. But I feel..." What? It was like being watched in a crowd. Someone not far away, thoughts fastened on her like staring eyes.

Skye was at the door, easing it open. "Wait!" Nora whispered.

"It's okay, you don't have to come." Skye gave her a little wave and stepped out.

Nora stood in the doorway, nervous. No moonlight reached the corridor. It was almost totally dark, except for the vague shape of Skye's white robe moving toward the stairs, pausing at the stair head, turning, moving down.

And then it hit her like a bad smell. The reason for her sense of danger, source of the calling voice, the clinging thoughts. It wasn't outside. It was inside.

It was in the house.

"Wait!" She made a dash for the stairs and slithered down. Skye was poised just above the little landing where you could see all the way to the lobby. She was putting out her foot to take another step down. Nora grabbed a silken sleeve and yanked her to a stop.

"What," Skye began, and then flinched. Nora looked where she was looking, at the bottom of the stairs.

A silvery light came in through the fanlight at the top of the front door and splashed across the newel post and the bottom three steps. Beyond this patch of silver the darkness was solid. At first Nora thought it was empty. Then she saw a hand resting on the newel post.

Not breathing, she traced the suggestion of an arm back to a tall man-shape, black on black. It lifted its face and looked at her with eyes like embers. Rage struck up at her.

"I told you to drown the talisman. You didn't. You failed me."

Go back, she whispered, but the words never left her lips. She couldn't stir, not even when the man-shape moved. Without taking a step, it suddenly stood higher. It was climbing the stairs.

"I thought you cared about me." His voice was still deep and soft as dark brown velvet, but cold as snow.

He stood on the third step now. Something about the arm that reached out to the railing suggested a short white sleeve. It occurred to her, even at the edge of panic, that she hadn't noticed his clothes before, only his face.

"That's right. I'm more like you now, Nora. Closer to life. Ike was a real help. You see? I'm getting stronger all the time."

Skye pressed hard against Nora's side, clamped both hands on her left arm and dug her nails in. They hurt. Nora hardly noticed. Adam had risen another step, and she saw that he was wearing a plain white T-shirt over dark jeans. So ordinary. But his burning eyes, they weren't ordinary at all.

"All it will take is one or two more lives," he said softly. "And then I'll be really alive, and free, and we can be together forever."

"Why are you doing this?" she whispered. "Why can't you leave me alone?"

His laughter shivered over her skin. "Because we have so much in common! We both drowned, didn't we?"

"But I—"

"The difference is, you came back to life, and I didn't. I stayed dead. How fair is that?"

"I didn't die!"

"Oh, but you did. Just for a little while. I can feel the dark place in your mind, down deep. That's what brought us together."

The fifth step now. Too close. What was to stop him coming all the way?

Scream, Nora ordered herself. Kick the railing. Take a step back. Break free! But her body never moved and her voice never sounded. Skye didn't move either, though her shivering shook Nora's body.

"Remember how it was?" His eyes shone. "I do. I remember all the time, every moment. What it was like to drown. The darkness. The choking. The terror."

Her throat closed. Inside her chest, her heart thudded, paused, thumped, fluttered. Her brain buzzed. She fought for breath.

His eyes, that's how he's doing it. "Skye, don't look at his eyes!" She forced her own eyes shut, the only movement she could make. But that was worse. In the night inside her head, he swooped at her.

She opened her eyes with a gasp. He stood just a step below the landing. One more step and he'd be within arm's reach. Darkness rose with him like a tide, chilling her feet and surging to stop her heart.

Chapter 21

A Crushed Blossom

JACK WAS HALFWAY down the stairs the next morning when a voice hissed at him from the second-floor corridor. When he looked back over the railing, Skye was beckoning from a narrowly opened door.

"In here!" she whispered piercingly, and opened the door wider. Nora looked at him over Skye's arm.

He came as far as the door. "I can't go in there. You know the rules. If Dr. Beth found out—" Skye grabbed his arm and yanked him inside. She slammed the door and leaned on it. Both girls were already dressed.

"Something happen?"

Nora looked at him with shadow-circled eyes. "Something."

"I saw it!" Skye planted herself in front of him. "With my own eyes, for the first time, I saw it!"

"Saw what?"

Her face crumpled. It looked like she hadn't brushed her hair this morning, just scraped it back into a careless ponytail. Which told him a lot about her state of mind. While she sat on her bed, hugging her knees and shivering, Nora, who seemed strangely calm, told him what they'd both seen last night.

"... and after locking the door and the window," she finished, "we took turns keeping watch. But nothing else happened."

"Hm..." Jack suppressed a shudder. So Adam had come right into the house. "It seems odd, though. Why did he stop?"

"I don't know," Nora said. "He reached the middle of the stairs, below the turn, and just stopped. And then he was gone."

"I've got a confession to make." Skye blotted her eyes and nose with the bed sheet. "All this time, I never really believed."

Nora stared. "You mean, in Adam?"

"In any of it." She waved her hands. "Crystals, dreams, running water, the occult. I studied it, I told myself I was serious, but it was all really just a game. Until last night."

"And now?"

"It's too much," she sniffled. "I can't cope. I'm going to call my parents and go home. Sorry, Nora, but—"

"Why should you worry?" Jack interrupted. "Adam's not the least bit interested in you. He wants Nora!"

"You're right." Skye's face cleared. Nora froze. Jack could have kicked himself for putting it that baldly.

But it was true. "It's Nora that should be leaving," he said firmly. The thought of her going away made a hollow place in his chest, but there was no other choice. She had to.

"I can't."

"But you can't stay here! Not when—"

She held up a palm. "After my mother worked and scrimped to pay for my time here? I can't throw that away."

"But if you told her..." He faltered.

"Yes? Tell her what? What could I say that wouldn't sound completely brain-damaged?"

"Let's work it out after breakfast. You'll both feel better with some food inside. So will I." He opened the door a crack, peeked through, opened it wider, poked his head out, looked both ways, and slipped out.

The corridor and stairwell were full of morning light. Smells of coffee and toast drifted up toward them. Jack decided to set an example of good sense and good cheer. "Isn't it hard to believe in ghosts and ghouls on a morning like this? Makes you think maybe it's all been just a bad dream, doesn't it?"

His good example fell flat. Neither girl said anything until they reached the bend in the staircase. Then Nora stopped and pointed. "See, this is where..."

Jack turned to see why she'd stopped, and found her looking down at the brown runner below her feet. A speck of vivid blue lay there in the middle of a patch of darker brown. When he looked close, it was a blossom. One of the tiny blue flowers, squashed flat.

"It must have come in on somebody's shoe." He bent to pick it up. His knuckles grazed the carpet. The fabric was sodden. Someone had stood there, someone who was soaked to the bone. Funny smell to it.... He sniffed his fingers. They smelled putrid. He stood up quickly, wiping his hand on his shorts, and decided not to mention that detail to Nora. Also to wash his hand as soon as possible.

"Leave the flower there," she said. "I think now I know why he never got higher than that."

They went on down the stairs, carefully avoiding the wet spot and the squashed flower. At the bottom Jack stopped and held up a hand. "Hey!"

Nora looked at him and then all around the lobby, warily. Skye said, "What?"

"There's one good thing. He said you'd let him down for not drowning the talisman, right? So that means it hasn't been neutralized, not yet!"

Nora's eyes brightened. "Right! That means..."

"It means," Jack said, "if we can find it, we still have a weapon!"

EVERY NERVE in Jack's body was alert for Adam's next appearance. But over that day and the two that followed — Friday, Saturday

125

and Sunday — life on Holdfast Island seemed to be back to normal.

Cuthbert came home from hospital and began hobbling about with the help of a cane. After spending Friday in a round of quizzes and tests, the whole school drove into Parry Sound for a pizza dinner and movie. On Saturday Beth led the six younger students on a geo-botanical field trip in the rugged hills of Killarney Provincial Park.

Sunday was a free day, but there was plenty to do. When Nora wasn't hiking in the woods, or learning how to handle a canoe, or forcing herself to swim lengths, she had her nose in a book. She never went near the ruined prison or the jail yard.

That wasn't so strange, Jack thought. And that she had so little to say to him, finding whatever she happened to be doing at any given moment far more fascinating than his company, he guessed that wasn't so strange either.

What was strange, in his opinion, was that she didn't appear to be looking for the talisman. Skye was, and he was: he'd poked into every nook, cranny, and hidey-hole where Bruce might have hidden the thing: he was still convinced that only Bruce could have taken and hidden it. He'd even found a way up into the cavernous and cob-webbed attic, and down into the furnace room, usually kept locked, and all over the greenhouse, and...

And all for nothing. But Nora hadn't lifted a finger to help search, far as he could tell. And he would have known; he had been keeping an eye on her, just in case Adam showed up.

On Sunday afternoon Jack caught up with her on the pier. She was sitting cross-legged in the sun, wearing that green swimsuit and a big straw hat, and reading a paperback novel: a mystery, judging by the cover.

"Hey, you're not that fish-belly white any more." Realizing that that wasn't much of a compliment he added, "You look nice." He spread out his towel beside her and sat down, folding up his long

126

arms and legs. Actually, he didn't think she looked nice. He thought she looked spectacular, with that wide-brimmed hat framing her dark hair and the green swimsuit sparking up the colour of her eyes.

She smiled at him and half-closed the book, keeping a finger in. Now was the time to find out if she had a boyfriend at home. Go ahead, he urged himself, ask! At that thought, a handsome, arrogant face drifted into his mind and the question asked itself.

"Have you seen Adam since Thursday?"

Her smile vanished. "I've decided there's no use thinking about Adam."

Which was not a straight answer. "Is he still getting into your dreams?"

"The flowers help." She closed her book and stood up.

He bounced up to keep her face at eye level. "Do you think those blue flowers are keeping him away? How? Where did they come from?"

"I have no idea."

"Well, what about the talisman? Shouldn't we all be looking for it?"

She started back toward the school.

"Don't you want to know the answers?" he yelled after her. "Don't you want to solve this?"

"It's not that simple!" she yelled back, and then ran.

"Oh, nicely done, Jack. Real smooth." He kicked the planks savagely. "You've scared her away completely!"

Chapter 22

Accident-Prone

HE WATCHED HER yank open the side door and disappear inside the school. It was clear what was going on here. Nora was trying to put some space between herself and the horrors of the last few days. Maybe she was trying to make herself believe that it was all over now, Adam was gone, things really were back to normal.

He could understand that, easily. There were things he wished he could put behind him, especially the memory of that wolf-like shape crouched over Ike. That shape had crawled into his dreams more than once. But it bothered him that she was putting him at a distance too.

"Well, might as well swim, now I'm here." His diving wasn't all that amazing, never had been. Better work on that unless he wanted Nora to laugh at him next time he tried it.

He stepped to the end of the pier, poised, and pushed off with his toes. On the push, his right foot slid in a wet patch and instead of slicing cleanly into the water, he cartwheeled in. Something stroked the back of his head on the way down. He surfaced and climbed out, spluttering and choking. Thank God she hadn't been there just then, to see him make a total fool of himself.

The back of his head smarted. Sitting on the pier with his feet in the water, he touched the place and his fingertips came away bloody. Hadn't felt like much. A shallow scratch, nothing to worry about. Must have just brushed the end of one of the planks when he fell. Then he looked at the solid wood under his hands and felt cold. Another half inch, and he might have knocked himself out. Then splosh, on in. And nobody around to see. *People drown that way.*

He got up and headed back toward the school, towelling himself as he went. "Got to be more careful," he muttered. This would make the third time in so many days that he'd come close to seriously hurting himself, or worse. "Thought I was past the clumsy stage. Guess not."

After changing back to shorts and T-shirt, he went looking for information about the blue flowers. Seeing Beth leaving her office, he asked her when the flowers first appeared, or had they always been around?

"No, they're something new, Cuthbert says. We first noticed them nineteen years ago, the year after..." Her face closed. Jack excused himself and backed off.

Today he couldn't say anything right!

"MELINDA?"

"Hi!" She looked up from a heap of potato peelings and surprised him with a grin. "You're too late for lunch and too early for dinner."

"Oh, I'm not here for food. Where's your helper?"

"Gone home early. It's Sunday."

"Can I do anything? I help my mother in the kitchen all the time. She says I'm a treasure."

"No kidding." She pointed her peeler at a stack of scrubbed carrots. "You could chop those into half-inch pieces. Use that cutting board and that knife. Put the pieces into that pot."

Jack stationed himself across the table from her, picked up a carrot and the knife, and started chopping. "Wow, this knife is really sharp."

"I keep all my knives sharp. Be careful." She stripped the potato of its skin with expert flicks of her peeler. "But you didn't come here to chop vegetables, did you? Not to ask after Zoe, neither."

"Well, to be honest, I'm trying to find out about Adam Sh—
Ow!" He dropped the knife and held up his left hand. A vigorous
stream of blood was flowing from a cut in the forefinger.

Melinda lunged around the table, grabbed him by the wrist and
hustled him across the room to the sink. She opened the cold water
tap and shoved his hand under the flow. "Stay there." A minute later
she was back with a first-aid kit. "All right, let's see it. Mm. It's
clean, and not as deep as I thought."

Jack felt slightly sick to see the blood welling again from the
whitened flesh. "I'm not usually this clumsy," he said, as she bound
the cut with gauze and tape.

"Well, stay away from knives in my kitchen, eh? I don't want to
be responsible for you losing a finger."

"I don't know what's the matter." Feeling a bit wobbly in the
legs, which was odd because he hadn't lost all that much blood, he
perched on a high stool near the table and watched as she started
cleaning mushrooms with a nubby cloth. "This is the fourth stupid
accident I've had in the last three days. That's not a bit like me."

"Oh? Accidents like what?" She shot a glance at him.

"Well, Friday I tripped on a stake in the garden and nearly put it
through my leg." He showed the bruise on his calf. "And yesterday
Hedda was reversing the truck and I stepped backwards into its path.
Bruce grabbed me just in time. And then today, I slipped on the end
of the pier and nearly hit my head. And then this. It's like I'm
jinxed!"

Her hands went on busily working, but her mouth was set. She
began to say something, thought better of it, closed her mouth.
Frowned, tried again. "Last time I heard of a boy who was suddenly
accident-prone was twenty years ago." She turned the mushroom
over in her fingers, peered at it, gave it a rub. "It was my first year
here. And my first-ever job. Cook's helper. I was just sixteen. Poor

Graham was always falling downstairs, or knocking his head on a branch. Once he fell down that bluff on the north side of the island, hurt his knee. Funny. He swore he wasn't usually that clumsy, just like you."

"Graham? Graham Newbury?"

"So you've heard of him."

"He was the boy who was killed that summer, hanged in the prison."

"That's right."

"I don't suppose he could've done that by accident."

"Nope."

"Melinda, what really happened that summer?"

She set down the mushroom and looked at him angrily. He held his breath, then let it out softly as she sat down on another high stool. "You were going to ask about Adam Shade. Why?"

"I know somebody who swears she's seen him."

She stared at him again, then surprised him by shrugging. "If anybody could cheat death, it would be Adam. He was clever — clever as Satan. He even won a scholarship to some famous American university. Harvard, I think it was."

That would account for some of the arrogance, Jack thought. But only some.

"He was different from other people. The way he talked — he could make you laugh till you cried. And then he'd say things that cut you off at the knees. He was dangerous."

There was a strange, faraway look on her face. Memories flickered across it. Jack wondered what Adam had meant to her. She'd been young then, young as Nora. "Why dangerous?" he asked quietly.

"Because he was so beautiful. Face like an angel. Voice like whiskey and honey. He could charm the heart out of you with a word.

And then he'd drop that little heart in the dirt and walk all over it. I called him an angel of darkness, and he just laughed at me."

"What made him like that, I wonder?"

She picked up another mushroom. "I've thought about that. I figure he took after his grandfather, from what I've heard. Bent crooked, both of them. Of course it didn't help that his mother treated him like he was the Angel Gabriel and Albert Einstein rolled into one! Gave him every single thing he wanted, whether it was good for him or not."

"Like what?"

"Like for instance, Hedda had a bunch of old knives and axes and guns that belonged to Governor Garvey. She used to tell me how valuable they were. I thought they were just sick. Things that people used to kill other people. But she let Adam have this fancy stick from the collection—"

"Stick?" Jack nearly fell off the stool.

"A sort of cane with a brass hawk's head. Looked like it could do damage. Adam liked to carry it, he'd swan around with this stick under his arm. Used to tell me it was more than it seemed."

"I suppose he thought it would impress the girls."

She sniffed. "It did, some of them." She gathered cleaned mushrooms in a heap and picked up a knife.

"Bet the other boys gave him a hard time over that."

"You'd think so, eh? But no, they steered clear. He had a way of looking at you..." Her voice grew thin. "Sometimes, when he was angry, there was a flicker in his eyes, like a little red flame. When you saw that, you backed off."

For a minute there was no sound in the kitchen but the soft click of Melinda's knife slicing through mushrooms to the wooden board beneath.

"Do you think he was insane?" Jack asked.

132

She mused on this, then slowly shook her head. "No. Or not in the usual way. He was always so cool and clever, always in control. He even planned the murders so as to confuse people as much as possible."

Jack felt breathless. "You mean, you know he did it? For sure?"

She lifted both shoulders. "Well, nothing was ever proved. Graham could've hanged himself, after killing Ursula. But if he did, where's the murder weapon?"

"Do they know what killed her?"

"Something long and sharp, like a long knife or a short, thin sword, the coroner said. But the blade was never found. You know what I think? I think Adam took it with him when he swam out across the bay, out into that storm. He drowned it when he drowned himself."

Her face sagged, and she looked older than she was. "Never mind, it's all ancient history now. But... funny thing. When I look back, the only face I remember clearly is his. Adam's."

Chapter 23

Darkness Gathers

BACK IN HIS ROOM, Jack fished the sword stick out of its hiding place. He had taped it behind the headboard of his bed. He had a strong feeling Melinda was right about most of what happened all those years ago, except what became of the murder weapon.

He pulled the blade out of its shaft and held it close to his eyes. Mindful of his strange new clumsiness, he handled it with utmost care. Where the steel blade met the brass collar you could see a thin line of black. Dirt, or old blood? Ursula's blood? And if it was, could it still be tested for DNA after twenty years? Only one way to find out.

"I've got to get this to the police!"

He slammed the blade back into the shaft, dashed out into the corridor and leaped down the stairs two by two. He would use the phone in Beth's office if she wasn't there. It was more private than the one in the common room.

Midway down the bottom flight, where the stairs curved on the little landing, his heel caught on the runner and down he went, rolling head over heels. He landed flat on his back on the hard tile floor at the base of the stairs and for a moment lay winded. He dragged air back into his lungs, meanwhile blinking up at the chandelier and trying to count how many copies of it were whirling around up there.

Vaguely, he sensed someone near.

"Hey! What happened? You all right?" Bruce's square face appeared above him.

Feet clattered on the stairs and Nora was bending beside Bruce. "Are you hurt?" She looked so frightened as she bent over him that he had to grin at her. "Just my pride, as usual."

Bruce stuck a hand down and helped Jack get to his feet. He flexed his arms and legs. "See? Nothing broken." Then he remembered the sword stick, and looked around. There was no sign of it.

"What happened to that stick I was carrying?"

"You mean," Nora said, "*the* stick?"

Jack nodded, watching Bruce. "That cane we dug up in the jail yard."

"I didn't see it," Bruce said sullenly.

"Well, maybe somebody else took it before you found me. Did you see anybody leaving?"

"There couldn't have been anybody else." Bruce scowled at him. "I was standing in the doorway of the common room. I heard somebody yell and I looked around and down you came like a ton of bricks. If anybody took your precious stick, they were invisible."

IT WAS CLOSE TO SUNSET when Nora walked down to the beach to find thinking space. There was no such space in her room, with Skye dancing dreamily around, tuned to whatever was flowing through her head via her earbuds.

At the pier she found most of the school, Jack included, playing a laughing, splashing game of water polo. Turning west along the beach, she walked along the sandy shore until the shouts and shrieks faded beyond the trees behind her.

So now the sword stick was gone, too. "Why?" She kicked at the sand. "What could he want with it? How could he use it?"

At the island's western point she climbed onto a spar of bleached timber, storm wrack from decades ago. Gazing out over the water at the setting sun, she thought back. What had he said, that night on the

135

stairs?

I'm getting more like you... closer to life... stronger all the time.

Strong enough, today, to hurt Jack. No, there was no way to prove it, but she was sure it was Adam who'd catapulted Jack down those stairs. He could have been killed — could have broken his neck.

Why? Why would Adam want to hurt Jack? Was it jealousy, or.... Wait. What else did he say? *Closer to life... Ike was a great help.*

She jumped off the spar and walked on, trying to sort out what Adam wanted, where he was taking them. He seemed to be the one in charge of what was happening, a scary thought to put it mildly.

And yet, since that night when he climbed the stairs and stepped on a blue-eyed flower, he hadn't come near her again. At least, not in her waking hours. Dreams were different. Always, these nights, she was travelling, walking down a dark path toward the sound of storm-driven waves breaking on a hidden beach. She had a companion on these walks, close at her side, someone she knew but could not see. He was always close to her by night.

But not by day. He was around, though. Often she'd feel a prickle on her neck or hear a whisper, and look up to see a human-shaped shadow under the eave of the woods, or a silhouette high on the ridge. Featureless at that distance, yet unmistakably Adam.

Nora's feet slipped on stone instead of sand. She caught her balance and looked around. Without meaning to, she'd walked all the way around to the north side of the island. The cliff rose behind her. Patches of the prison wall showed through the trees on the crest, the stones red in the sunset light.

Chilled, she turned to go back, then stopped. A dark figure stood up from the base of the cliff and in two steps was blocking her path. Nora backed away.

"I often come here, just to sit and look at the water," said Hedda

Shade. "You know what happened here, don't you?" She tilted her head toward the bay, without taking her eyes off Nora's face.

"Y-yes." Nora tried to sidestep past her, but somehow Hedda was in her way again.

"I know what they say happened. But they never found his body. You know that too, don't you?"

Nora nodded, watched her warily, tensed, ready to run.

"I never really believed he was gone," Hedda said quietly, as if to herself. The silence filled with the *shush, shush* of small waves on the rocks. Then, still more quietly: "You've seen him, haven't you?"

Nora flinched. A light leaped into Hedda's eyes. "So I was right!"

"No!"

"Yes! He's alive and you know it!"

"He's not alive!" Nora splashed past her into the water and out again. She ran, swift with terror, while behind her a scream rose up.

"Where is he?"

Her wet feet skidded on smooth rock and she fell, scrambled up, ran, fell again. At the island's point she stopped, panting, and looked back. There was no sign of Hedda. But as she walked on, she kept turning her head to look back. When she came within sight of the jetty, the game of water polo was still in progress.

JACK GROANED, rolled over, and sat up. He hadn't slept much. It's hard to sleep when you're aware that there's a possibility, no matter how remote, that the person in the next bed might get up in the night and start walking around under the control of someone or something else. Suppose that someone/something told your roomie to stick a long, sharp knife in you?

Bruce was snoring again. That didn't encourage sleep, either. Bruce at his worst sounded like a Mack truck revving its engine.

Muttering, Jack got up and went to look out of the window. One of the first things he'd noticed after Nora arrived at the school was that his room was almost directly above hers. He had thought of tying amusing notes to a string and dangling them in front of her window. But that had been before this Adam saga started, before people were hurt and killed. Amusing notes now seemed out of place.

Shoving up the screen, he stuck his head out and looked down. From here, Nora's window was lost in a cloud of the blue-flowered vines. Funny how they stopped there and came no higher.

Unnatural! She was right. This whole scene was wrong. On the surface, things looked normal on the island. But underneath, something was sneaking up on Nora and him and all of them. Something... well, he hadn't ever before in his life seriously used the word "evil", but that was what seemed to fit, here and now. Something evil creeping up on them.

He pulled his head in and was about to lower the screen when movement caught his eye. Who was that out there, walking past the greenhouse? He squinted, and made out a solid, compact figure with hair that gleamed like steel in the moonlight. Hedda Shade.

She wasn't alone. As she walked on past the greenhouse and started up the path that led up the hill toward the woods, Jack made out a tall figure, looked like a man, walking beside her. He held something in his hand, some stick, and was slashing at the grass with it as he walked.

Jack's hands tightened on the sill. Should he warn her? Yell out the window? Would she listen? He dithered a moment, then grabbed the flashlight from his dresser and tiptoed downstairs. He let himself out the side door without making a noise.

But he was too late. Although he ran barefoot as far as the prison wall, he saw no one. He shouted Hedda's name. No answer came back except the cry of a night bird circling high above.

138

Chapter 24

The Hangman's Maze

AFTER BREAKFAST Jack went back to his room for his notebooks. First class of the day was chemistry, led by the supply teacher, Mr. Quinn, who'd been filling in for Dr. Cuthbert. Downstairs again, he was on his way along the corridor leading to the classroom wing when he passed Beth's office. The door was open. Her voice reached him.

"It's just that I'm a little worried. Hedda's always so reliable. She wouldn't go off like this without telling me."

Jack stopped. His spine suddenly felt cold.

"I understand," Beth said. "Yes, I see your point. It would be premature. Goodbye, then." A telephone clattered. Beth sighed.

Jack knocked on the door jamb and stepped inside. "Sorry, I couldn't help hearing. About Mrs. Shade? Is something wrong?"

Beth cocked her head, studied him a moment, then made up her mind. "I hope not. She hasn't been seen since last night, that's all. Her bed hasn't been slept in. And she hasn't taken the truck or the car."

"Maybe she walked into the village."

"I've checked with the coffee shop and the general store, the only two places she could have gone. Nobody's seen her. And she doesn't have friends there. The police say they don't see any reason yet to mount a search. She's fit, competent and adult, she hasn't been missing very long, and the weather's clement." She added, "They're right, there's no reason to worry, not yet." But she sounded worried.

139

"I saw her last night. I mean, early morning."

"You did?" Beth straightened up.

"Yes, but she wasn't going towards the bridge." He told her what he'd seen from his window; but decided not to mention his impulsive barefoot search. In plain daylight, it sounded hare-brained.

Beth whistled soundlessly. "Sounds odd, somehow. Did you recognize this man?"

"He... he was just a shadow. Tall. Except for that, I couldn't see much."

"Mm." She cleared her throat and gazed meditatively out the window. Plenty worried, he thought, but not willing to let him see that. "Perhaps I'll take a walk over in that direction."

"I'll go with you." He dumped his books on the sofa in the corner. "Suppose she's fallen and hurt herself? You'd need help."

For a moment he thought she was going to refuse. Then she nodded sharply. "Let's go, then." She went to the desk, pulled two heavy flashlights out of a drawer and handed him one.

Bruce was passing the door of the office as they came out. Beth touched his arm. "Tell Mr. Quinn that Jack is excused from his first class, please, Bruce."

They headed out the side door, along the house and up the hill toward the woods, with Jack shortening his long stride to match Beth's.

NORA BENT OVER the heavily pencilled and much-erased page of her workbook, but nothing there made sense. "Draw the Lewis Structure for ammonia" might as well have been printed in Klingon.

Her eyes kept drifting to Jack's empty chair. As the minutes dragged on, she worried. Maybe he was sick. Maybe he'd got bad news from home. Maybe he'd had an idea about what Bruce might have done with the talisman, and skipped class to go looking for it.

140

Couldn't he have waited for me?

Someone cleared his throat loudly nearby. She looked up to see Mr. Quinn frowning down at her. He looked at the clipboard in his hand, then back at her. "Nora Brook, is it? Well, Nora, I'd be most grateful if you'd condescend to give a fraction of your attention to this class. That's twice I've asked you a question without getting an answer."

"Um, sorry. I'm... um, tired, I guess."

"Hm. Maybe so. You look it. Well, everybody take a five-minute break. Get up, have a stretch." He walked away. Nora shoved back her chair and crossed the room to where Bruce was sitting. He was opening a copy of *Sports Illustrated* on top of his workbook.

He looked up when she dropped into the chair across the table from him. Instantly his eyes twitched away from hers. Nervous, she thought. Or guilty. On impulse, she pointed an accusing finger. "All is discovered! Confess!"

He scowled at her from under his blond eyebrows, then bent over the magazine.

"Come on, where is it?"

"Where's what?"

She bent low to hiss. "The snake ring! Where did you hide it?"

He darted another look at her, then his eyes switched away. "Don't ask."

"You mean you really—"

"Just don't ask."

He knew something. It must have been him that stole the talisman, just as they'd suspected. But there was something more, Nora thought, staring at him. There was something different about him.

He hunched over the magazine and tried to pretend she wasn't there. As she watched him, it came to her. He was like a rabbit flattening itself to the ground, pretending to be invisible, willing the

141

hawk's eyes not to see.

Bruce, all 200 pounds of him, was quivering with fear.

"Tell me what's wrong," she whispered.

He shook his head.

"Then at least tell me why Jack's not in class."

"He went to help Dr. Beth with something."

"Went? Where?"

"Dunno. They had flashlights. They went outside."

Flashlights. Outside, in the middle of the day. That could mean only one place.

Nora bounced up and was out the door before Mr. Quinn could call her back. As she ran past the greenhouse toward the hill path, someone angrily yelled her name. She raced on.

"RULE NUMBER ONE, when exploring sinister deserted ruins," Jack advised himself aloud. "Don't split up!"

He swung the flashlight beam over walls where plaster had crumbled off in chunks, exposing the rough stones underneath. They looked exactly like the walls he'd passed ten minutes ago. And exactly like the walls he'd passed five minutes ago.

"And rule number two," he went on, deliberately loud and cheerful, "don't lose your sense of direction. I wouldn't have thought that was possible in a building like this. I mean, it's big, but it's not that complicated, right? It's basically a shoebox."

Impossible as it seemed, he was lost. He and Dr. Beth had started by exploring all of the main floor of the prison — grimy, empty offices, corridors lined with open bars, a filthy-looking kitchen where small animals (mice?) pattered away from the light, making him jump.

Then Beth had sent him up to search the second and third floors, while she took the stairs down to the lower cellblock levels. He had spent ten minutes opening every door on the second level and finding nothing but dust, fallen plaster, and the odd rusty paperclip. Some of the rooms had windows: most looking outward into the woods, a few looking inward, into the dark void of the cellblock well.

It was only as he was climbing the stairs to the top floor that he noticed footprints in the dust. One set of prints, going up. None coming down. Prints made by feet about.... He set one sneakered foot beside the mark on the stair. Smaller than his, but not by much. About Hedda's size, he estimated.

Up, but not down. So that meant.... He thought of going to find Beth, then shook his head and kept climbing. Find Hedda first, see what the score was, then tell Beth.

The third floor was different from the two below. There were no marks that showed there had ever been any furniture on these floors, no nail holes in the walls. "I'm willing to bet they never used this level at all," Jack muttered. "So what was it for?"

As on the second floor, a few of the rooms had windows, but they were tiny and crusted with dirt. Some were broken, and the rooms were fouled with bird droppings and old squirrel nests, the floors under the windows drifted with composting leaves. Jack found a tiny, stunted pine tree rooted in one such heap and struggling toward the light.

Two doors beyond that, he stepped into a room filled with greenish light. The window was overgrown with vines, the ones with the blue-eyed flowers. The glass was half gone and the vines had crept in. Some of them reached almost to the doorway.

"Give them another year or so and they'll cover the whole building." The thought cheered him. He imagined a huge shoebox-shaped block of bright green and heavenly blue where the sad old stones of the prison used to be.

He left the doors of these rooms standing open, so that a little light leaked into the corridor from the windows. Hedda's trail, if it was hers, was easy to follow. But as he turned corner after corner, he began to wonder.

When he saw that he was following a double set of prints, and the second set was his own, he stopped. The echoes of his footsteps pattered away into an impossible distance.

"She must have been wandering around and around," he decided aloud, needing his own voice for company. "And she must have gone into some side passage I didn't notice. Or some room. Who knows, maybe she's in one of these rooms... um, what for? Meditating? Camping out?"

He swung the flashlight beam around and back. The door to the stairwell should be about here. But it wasn't. No side corridor, either. And ahead —

As the beam hit the end of the corridor, a dark shape flicked around the corner and was gone.

"Hedda! Wait!"

He set off at a run. When he reached the corner the hallway ahead was empty. But about halfway along, to the right, was a narrow corridor that he'd somehow missed until now. When he reached that spot and flashed his light along the corridor's length, something — the edge of a hand, maybe — was just slipping around the corner at the far end.

He set off again, but not running this time and not shouting. He walked warily, swinging the beam from side to side. At each doorway he carefully eased the door open and edged just his head in. Then stepped in when it seemed safe. Flashed his light into the corners, looked for marks in the dust, found none. Sidled out, glancing both ways.

So Hedda was leading him on a chase. Playing with him. Something wrong with her, obviously. *I always did think she was kind of strange.*

Corner after corner. The corridors seemed endless. He felt as if he'd walked miles. And still the echoes ran away into an impossible distance. And again and again the hint of a dark figure, a sleeve or a heel or the hem of a jacket, kept teasing him on. It was a bad dream, except he knew he was awake.

He stopped again. Time to call it quits. Time to go find Beth. Whatever was happening here broadcast a strange, jangling vibe, a kind of madness. It was out of his league. To be honest, it scared him silly.

He looked back and forth along the corridor, and it occurred to him that he hadn't seen the door to the stairs in a long while. But of course it had to be there. He just had to keep walking.

At the next corner, he found himself at last in a place he hadn't been before: a long hallway with no doors on either side. The walls were bare stone that had never been plastered. It ended in a wall pierced by a small eye-shaped window, a flattened oval, the only break in all that stone. As he got closer to the end, the grey light that found its way through the grimy glass showed small green pillows of moss on the stones and cobwebs stirring in the angles between walls and ceiling. Small, many-legged critters scurried into cracks as he passed.

"Guess I didn't know when I was well off, before." He laughed, and malicious echoes laughed back at him. He bit it off. The echoes giggled into silence.

Under the oval window the shadows, by contrast with the meagre light, lay blacker than ever. As he walked nearer, he made out a shapeless form huddled against the end wall. He stopped, his heart thumping. Swallowed hard a couple of times. Walked on slowly. When he was within three strides his light picked out Hedda's steel-coloured hair and dusty green workman's pants and shirt.

"Hedda?" She didn't answer. She sat as if she'd slid down the wall and slumped there, exhausted, her chin on her chest. Maybe she got lost too, he thought. "Hedda? You okay?" She didn't stir, didn't look up, didn't speak.

She seemed to be cradling a shiny object in her hands against her shirt. Jack stepped closer, aiming the light. It was a long moment before he realized the shiny object was a brass hawk's head. It took a full minute before his mind allowed him to see that she was not exactly holding the hawk's head, and still longer before he questioned where the rest of the Hangman's sword stick was hidden.

When he understood, he leaped back. Cold iced him from the inside out. He took another step back, keeping the light on Hedda. He could not turn around and go. Suppose she raised her head and looked at him, suppose those empty eyes touched his back? Suppose she got up, silent, and...

Another step back, the beam swinging. Another. Then something blocked him. He was pushing back against something he couldn't either feel or resist, air turned to jelly.

Then, in the dead light from the oval window, he saw a wooden panel set in the floor at his feet. And in the panel, the square shape of a trap door. And a thick loop of rough rope that hung in the air before his eyes. Things that had not been there before.

While his mind fought with gut instinct, screaming that none of this could be happening, the force behind him shaped itself into hands that locked around his wrists, pulled his arms behind his back, and rushed him at the noose.

Chapter 25

Hunt in Darkness

THE PRISON DOOR hung open, but it was festooned with loops of the blue-flowered vines. New vines: they had grown luxuriantly over the gap since the last time she'd been there. Nora reached out to push them aside. Then hesitated, her hand in the air.

One blossom on the stairs had stopped him.

Unless, of course, that had only been coincidence.

Oh, what harm could it do? She broke off a foot-long creeper so thickly covered with flowers that it was like a blue plume; then another, then a third, and held them together in a waving bouquet. Then she lifted the rest of the vine curtain and ducked inside.

"Jack! It's me, Nora!"

No answer, nothing but a whisper of wind far away. The building echoed. It sounded a lot bigger than it really was. "Jack! Dr. Beth! Are you in here?" Still no answer.

"Dumb," she muttered. "No flashlight, no notion of where they might be. How will I find them?" Better go back. Get lights, get help.

No. By then it might be too late. It might already be too late. Danger pricked at her nerves. *Move!*

Okay, okay. That voice in her head spoke sense. She guessed it was the sensible side of her brain, whichever side that was, speaking up through the noisy chaos of fear.

She took in air, trying not to breathe through her nose, and moved toward the rectangle of blackness that she recalled as the door that led to the first level of cells, and the stairwell. In the greenish light that struggled in past the vines, that was all she could see.

Jack and Beth had flashlights, she remembered. No doubt she'd spot their lights when she got close. She'd hear them, too.

Setting each foot down with care in the semi-dark, she crossed the entrance room, hesitated on the threshold of darkness, and then stepped across. She took two steps into pitch blackness, and stopped again.

She was paralyzed. The darkness was a living thing pressing against her. It took every scrap of will power she could scrape up to shove terror back into the corner where it belonged.

Hurry!

The best way to go forward was to reach out and touch the rows of bars along the front of the cells, and use them as a guide. Then at least she wouldn't walk smack into things, or fall down the stairwell.

With her right hand still clutching the spray of vines, she stretched her left hand out to the side. It met something cold but soft, something that moved against her hand, curled to grip....

Her scream echoed down the corridor. She was blind, suffocating, deafened by her own pounding heartbeat.

Hold on!

When her eyes cleared, it seemed not as dark as it had been. The bars of the nearest cells were visible as bluish strokes on black. Nothing moved behind them. Nothing there, not now, she told herself. Nothing.

"My eyes must be getting used to the dark," she said shakily, trying to put a smile in her voice. "Hey, I can even see the flowers."

The flowers, in fact, were plain to see in the dark. Each petal looked like a tiny window on the sky.

It was then she realized that whatever light there was came from the flowers. And as she took one cautious step after another, they glowed brighter. Bright enough to take her quickly to the stairwell door at the end of the corridor. She stopped wondering and kept moving.

But now where? "Jack! Dr. Beth!" An answer came from below: a faint call, so faint she wasn't sure whether she had imagined it. She started down the stairs, then stopped. The flowers were fading, leaving her in the dark again. Another step down left her in total darkness.

Hastily feeling her way up to the landing again, Nora found the light brightening around her again. A clear signal.

"All right. Up we go."

The flowers became her guide. At the next landing the fading of the light told her that what she wanted was not on the second floor. Up again. As she climbed, she felt a moment's doubt.

"I'm crazy to put this much trust in these unnatural things. How do I know where they come from? Or what they want? They could be leading me into a trap."

But it was too late to back out now. The prickling of her nerve-endings told her that time was running short.

Hurry!

Was that voice really in her own head, or did it come from somewhere else? She reached the third-floor landing and stepped into a corridor that smelled more like a cave in the woods than a building. Something in the air made her feel sick. What was it? All it smelled of was dampness and earth and animals, as if human beings had never come here.

Hurry! Hurry!

She held the cluster of flowers out at arm's length, like a blue torch, and swung it slowly in an arc. To the right it faded. To the left it brightened, showing a hallway with open doors stretching into dimness. Nora started running.

Straight ahead, then left. Then right, along a narrow corridor.

149

Left again. All the while, the sick feeling grew inside her. It came to a head when she turned into a long corridor with an eye-shaped window at the end.

Against the grey light from the window, dark shapes moved. Nora forced terror back one more time and flung herself forward. But each foot seemed to take five minutes to rise and fall. What was happening at the end of the corridor would be done before she could get there.

"Jack!"

His body was twisted, arms straining behind him. His feet were lifting from the ground. No, not lifting. The floor was opening under him, a widening gap like a mouth opening to howl.

Nora took the last two metres in a flying leap. As their bodies collided, the sharp smell of the flowers exploded around them. The one grey eye of the window became two scarlet embers, and then winked out.

Chapter 26
School Closing

"I THINK, NOW, I understand." Nora used Jack's flashlight to trace the outline of the trapdoor at her feet. The flowers lay on it in a heap, their glow faded to nothing. "They only used this level for one thing."

The cracks around the square trap were solid with dust. Looking at it, you knew it hadn't budged in half a century. In the ceiling above, only a rusty stain showed where a pulley might have been fastened, decades ago. And yet there was no doubt at all in her mind that if she had arrived two seconds later, Jack would be hanging there, and he'd be as dead as the figure huddled under the window.

Jack knew it too. He was shaking like a poplar leaf. He sat on the stone floor with his arms clasped around knees that were not yet firm enough to hold him up.

He rubbed his throat, swallowed painfully, and tried, for the third time, to speak. "How... find me?"

"I had help."

He looked a question.

"Remember that night we dowsed for the sword stick? When I felt there were other people with us in the garden, two wills struggling against each other, and we were caught in the middle? Well, I think it happened again. One of them was with me."

Nora looked at Hedda's folded shape, and was glad she couldn't see her face. The brass bird's head was caked and dull in places, but the black crystal of its eye glittered.

"Got... tell Beth," Jack croaked.

151

Leaning on her shoulder, he lurched to his feet. They staggered together to the stairs and laboriously made their way down. As they reached the ground floor, they met Beth coming up. A streak of blood smeared her cheek.

"You're hurt!" Nora cried.

"Not badly. I slipped on the steps and knocked myself silly for a minute, that's all. This place really is a menace!" Then she stopped and played her light over their faces. "What happened to you two? You look as if you've been dragged through a hedge backwards."

"We found Hedda," Jack said huskily. "I wish we hadn't."

"I DON'T LIKE coincidences. And three is just too many." Staff Sergeant Wilbert Rose, O.P.P Parry Sound, had eyes as hard and grey as the local granite, and those eyes stayed steady on Jack's face. They rested on Nora's face, too. But mostly on mine, Jack thought.

He was glad that Dr. Beth and Dr. Cuthbert had ranged themselves side-by-side behind the desk, and given the policeman a chair in front, just like any visitor. It meant they weren't handing over their authority.

Jack was feeling vulnerable. He'd been feeling that way ever since he fell out of a nightmare and landed beside a hangman's drop — and found himself still in a nightmare.

Nora hadn't said much, but she looked and sounded braver than he felt. The two of them sat to the left of the desk, facing Staff Sgt. Rose, on chairs carried in from the classroom.

"Coincidences," Rose said again, tapping a thick finger on his blue serge-covered knee. "You were both there when Dr. Loftus was hurt. You were both there when Ike Frey died. And now Hedda Shade's dead, and there you are again, the two of you."

"Don't forget, Staff Sergeant, the first instance was an accident, one they couldn't have predicted." Cuthbert thumped his cane on the

152

floor and tried to sound hearty. "And as you can see, I'm far from dead!"

Beth's voice was crisp. "In Ike's case, the cause was natural: a heart attack. That's been confirmed."

Then an awkward pause.

Rose smiled tightly. "But there's nothing natural about Mrs. Shade's death, is there?"

"Well, no — obviously." Cuthbert's hands tightened on his cane. "We knew she was unhappy, but we had no idea she was as troubled as all that."

"Suicide?" The policeman's bushy eyebrows went up. "I'm not so sure. You'd have to be pretty damn determined, to shove a blade clear through your rib cage."

"That's enough!" Beth shot to her feet, and Cuthbert lurched up to stand beside her.

"Not in front of the children, you mean?" Rose stood up too. "Well, they aren't exactly children, are they? I still want to ask them some questions. Like, why Miss Brook, here, ran off to the prison as soon as she found out her friend had gone that way. You'd think she was expecting trouble."

Nora opened her mouth, but Beth hushed her with a gesture. "No questions without their parents present."

"We've been trying to contact their parents."

Jack shot a horrified look at Nora. *My folks'll go ballistic!* She shot the same look back.

"The McKies," Rose went on, "are at some scientific conference in England. Mrs. Brook is in a hospital in Ottawa."

"Hospital?" Jack grabbed Nora's hand. "What's the matter?"

"Chill, she's a nurse." Nora gave Rose a furious look. "She can't just up and leave her shift!"

"Fair enough," he said. "But they'll all be here tomorrow, next day at latest. Then we'll talk."

"We're letting the other students go home today," Beth said.

Rose looked as if he was going to argue, then he shrugged. "So long as I have their contact information." He nodded impartially at the Loftuses, gave Nora a sharp look and Jack a sharper one, slapped his cap back on and marched out of the room.

Cuthbert sank back into his chair. Beth came out from behind the desk and paced nervously.

"You're letting the others go home?" Nora repeated.

"That's right. We're closing the school, just for this summer, and refunding all fees." Cuthbert tried to smile, but didn't quite make it.

Jack was stabbed with guilt. "Because of what happened to you?"

"Not just that. Everything. What happened to Hedda was the last straw." He shook his head. "Nobody can learn or teach properly in an atmosphere like this."

SKYE SNAPPED the locks of another suitcase and carried it to the doorway, where it became part of a matched set of four. "For your sake I wish I could stay, but I can't. My mother's hysterical."

Nora watched from her perch at the end of her bed. "Don't let it bother you. I'll be okay." She'd washed, changed her dust-smeared shorts and T-shirt for clean ones, and told herself she'd recovered from what happened in the jail this morning. But she didn't feel recovered, and Skye was too sharp to miss that.

"I wish you could come home with us for a few days! I hate to think of you here all by yourself."

"I won't be alone. I'll have Jack."

"Oh — Jack!" Skye cast her eyes to heaven and waved him away.

"And besides, I couldn't just leave. Not only because the police say I can't, but — well, after what we did."

154

"Look, Nora." Skye sat down on the bed and gripped both her hands. "This isn't your mess. Even if it were, it's too messy for you to deal with. Too dangerous."

"Who will, then, if I don't?" Nora got up, to avoid further argument, and picked up one of Skye's heavy suitcases. "I'll take this down."

She lugged the case down the stairs and out the front door, to where a taxi was waiting in the hot noon sunshine. Back inside, she was about to head up the stairs again when a tall, heavy figure barred her way.

"Got something you should see," Bruce said.

Nora just stopped herself from taking a step back. She had never liked Bruce, she'd only tolerated him for Skye's sake. There was always something about him that made her think of a glacier: cold and massive and indifferent.

"Well, what?"

"C'mon." He wrapped his fist around her arm and walked her down the corridor. If she'd had time to think she might have yelled or struggled, but surprise kept her quiet until they reached the door of the Loftuses' office. Then she pulled free.

"What the heck do you want?"

His pale eyes slid over hers. "I just want out of here. But I figure I should tell you about my dream, first." He pushed open the door and walked in. Nora hesitated, then followed. She made sure the door stayed open.

"What dream?"

"Thursday afternoon, it was hot, so I went upstairs for a nap. Next thing I knew, I was up again. But it was like..." He gestured helplessly. "Nothing was normal. I went to Jack's dresser and pulled out one of the drawers and took this thing that was stuck to the bottom."

155

"The talisman!"

"Whatever. A round gold thing wrapped in plastic. Anyway, I took it. I went downstairs and out the door and up the hill to the woods. All the time, it was like it wasn't me. I just hung in there and watched."

Nora stared at him, horrified. "The talisman. What did you do with it?"

"I'm telling you. I got to that spring in the woods and I opened the plastic bag and I took the thing out. I held it out over the water. I knew that was what I was supposed to do. And then..." He rocked back and forth on his heels.

Nora clenched her hands. She breathed in hard through her teeth.

"Then I woke up," Bruce said simply.

"And?"

"I was too scared to think. When I started thinking, I knew what I had to do. And I did it."

"If you don't tell me right this instant—"

"That's why I brought you here. I figure you'll know what to do with the thing, sooner or later."

"Bruce!" She grabbed him by the arms and tried to shake him. It was like shaking an oak tree. "What did you do with it?"

"Check the Bible." He shrugged free and walked out.

Chapter 27

Closer to Life

NORA STOOD ALONE in the silent room, collecting her thoughts. Then she looked around. The walls were lined with shelves, and the shelves were crammed with books. Behind Dr. Cuthbert's desk was a glass-fronted cupboard where rich-looking bindings gleamed behind diamond-patterned leading.

"That must be where they keep their expensive books."

In part, she was right. But the sole Bible in the cupboard was the shabbiest book of the collection. It looked as if somebody had read and re-read it many times. Or more than one somebody.

With delicate care, Nora turned the tissue-soft pages. In the middle was a section of heavier paper headed "Births, Marriages and Deaths," and filled with the handwritten names of generations of Loftuses. The last name written down was "Ursula."

There was nothing between the pages, of course. The talisman wouldn't fit there, small through it was. Nora closed the book. Check the Bible, Bruce said. Was there another one? She stood running her eyes along the shelves, meanwhile holding the tattered book in her left hand, the spine against her palm.

The spine was lumpy.

Nora smiled. She opened the Bible wide and tilted it up, and the snake ring slid out.

"AND WHAT DID YOU do with it?" Jack asked. Nora took a hand from her pocket and opened her fingers. Gleaming in the mid-after-

157

noon sun, every tiny snake-scale perfectly incised, it was a beautiful thing. And yet as evil, in its way, as that razor-sharp blade inside the Hangman's cane. She quickly slipped it back into the pocket of her shorts.

Jack laughed. "Bruce wasn't as dumb as he looked, eh? He hid it in the one place where he figured it was guaranteed to be safe!"

They were sitting in a patch of meadow grass on the hillside overlooking the road. Below them, the last of the taxis rolled dustily toward the bridge. Beth brought up the rear with the pickup truck, driving Melinda and Zoe into the village. Jack waved as they went by. Melinda, sitting in the box with the luggage, waved back.

When the bridge had stopped its hollow rumbling and the dust drifted away, Nora stood up, skidded down to the road, and trudged back toward the school. Jack walked beside her, hands in pockets, kicking bits of gravel.

Well, here they were. Nora and himself almost alone on the island, and no classes. He drew a breath. There would never be a better time. *Go for it!*

"Nora, um, d'you think maybe we could, you know, see each other after we leave here?" It came out less casual and more crammed-together than he'd intended.

She gave him a quick glance. "See each other? You mean, meet? How could we? Toronto's what, five hundred miles from Ottawa?"

"Yes, but we could keep in touch. Texting. We could write every day if we wanted!" He stopped and fumbled in a pocket of his shorts. Found a gel pen and a small notebook, wrote on one page, and tore it out. "There, that'll get me." He handed her the page. "Why are you shaking your head?"

"Because it's impossible." She folded the page sadly and handed it back to him. "It just can't happen."

His heart sank. "But..." He struggled to find the right words.

Then to his amazement, he saw she was grinning. "I don't have anything to text with, you idiot!"

"You're kidding!"

"Nope. Mom's against those kinds of things. Cool devices. She's convinced smart phones give you brain cancer. I just have regular email. And I guess good old pen and paper, too." Her eyes sparkled at him. "Hey, I like that idea, don't you? Real letters, with stamps on. Here, give me that notebook." She took it from him and wrote something, then handed it back. "That's my address, e- and snail."

He suddenly felt like a bubble in a glass of fizzy ginger ale. The afternoon turned golden. He whooped and punched at the sky, and Nora lit up with laughter.

Then a shadow crossed her face. "Jack, I'm sorry."

"Sorry! For what?"

"I've been pushing you away these last few days. Because I was so scared. You wanted to do something about Adam, and I just wanted to hide my head in the sand."

"I wondered for a while if maybe he was gone for good. I hoped so."

She shook her head, then dug in another pocket and brought out a sprig of blue flowers. It looked surprisingly fresh. "I always carry some of these, so maybe that's why he's stayed away from me. But I've often seen him at a distance. And always, always, in my dreams."

She shivered. Jack wrapped a hand around hers. "I wish," he said, "we could persuade Dr. Beth and Dr. Cuth to drape themselves with those flowers, but somehow I can't see that happening."

She started toward the school again. "Maybe I could tuck little sprigs into their pockets, secretly. Like I did in yours."

"What?" He stopped and felt in his other shorts pocket and brought out a crushed bit of green and blue. Even as it lay on his palm it unfolded and fluffed out. "Well, I'll be hornswoggled. You're like Mata Hari!"

She laughed again, then let the smile slip. "It's not much, but I have to try to do something. I mean, with Adam lurking around like a man-eating tiger."

"You mean, we have to do something!" He swung her hand energetically. He was bursting with good feelings. At that moment he could have could pulled the ears of a dozen man-eating tigers.

"It's my fault this happened." She looked stubborn. "If I'd left the stick buried, Adam would probably not be able to walk around like that, and hurt people, like he hurt Ike. And you. At most he'd be a, a puff of wind, a shadow, a thing with no real power."

"It wasn't your fault. Anybody could have found the stick."

"I'm not so sure about that. Anyway, it was me. And that set things going. Don't you see the pattern?"

He did, and it made him feel cold inside. "It started with Dr. Cuth."

"No, it started with you. Right away. Remember the hawk's beak?" She lifted his hand. A half-healed cut showed on the back. "Then Cuthbert was hurt. Then Ike died. Something worse each time, and each time he's been growing stronger. Closer to life, he said. Killing Hedda must have been easy for him."

"To kill his own mother..." He hunched his shoulders and shivered. "Melinda called him an angel of darkness, and she was right."

"Jack, if he kills one more time he'll be strong enough to go anywhere he wants, I'm sure of it. And who's to stop him if I won't try?"

He pulled her to a halt just within sight of the school. A memory of strong, cold hands on his wrists and a rough rope at his throat brought back the sickness and terror. "Nora, there's no way you can stop him. Keep away from him, for God's sake!"

"But I've got to try something, before he takes another life! All I

160

can think of is to bury the talisman in the garden again, and hope it keeps him bound there."

"It may not work. Even if it does, sooner or later he'll make sure somebody else digs it up again."

"Yes, but that might be years from now. By then, maybe, we'll have found out what to do. Anyway, it's the only thing I can think of."

"Whatever you do, count me in." They set off along the road again. "Don't shut me out. Okay?"

"I won't. I promise." Her smile was almost enough, he thought, to make up for the place in his chest that still felt sick and cold.

AS THEY CUT ACROSS the meadow to the school, a curtain moved in one of the ground-floor windows and a face looked out. It smiled at Nora, then drew back, and the curtain closed.

She stopped short. "That's Dr. Cuth and Dr. Beth's office."

Jack's hand tightened. "And that wasn't Dr. Cuth." He dropped her hand and was off at a dead run, with Nora at his heels. They burst through the front door, raced along the corridor and in through the open door of the office.

Cuthbert sat slumped in the chair behind his desk. His head was tilted to one side, his eyes were closed and he was breathing heavily. Adam stood behind him, hands set lightly on Cuthbert's shoulders. The pose looked affectionate. He smiled at them over Cuthbert's shaggy head.

Jack muttered under his breath, clenched his fists, and started toward him.

"Wait!" Nora caught his wrist. "Look!" She pointed. The glass-fronted cupboard behind the desk mirrored the room and everything in it: including Cuthbert, and herself, hand outstretched, and Jack with both fists clenched and ready.

161

But not Adam. In the glass, Cuthbert's reflection was alone. Nothing stood behind it.

"That's right." Adam's smile was all for Nora. "I'm not quite there — not yet. But don't think that means I can't kill Cuthbert, because I can."

"You disgusting monster," Jack said quietly. His fists were still up. He pulled loose from Nora's hand and started forward.

"Take one more step," Adam said, "and his heart stops."

Chapter 28

Doors to Death

JACK PULLED UP, breathing hard. "No! You can't!" Nora cried.

"Why not?" Adam lifted a shoulder. "There's already been lots of death in this room. Besides, he would deserve it. He tried to keep me and Ursula apart. And look what came of that!"

She wet her lips. "What do you want?"

"Just to talk with you. Just to be with you. I thought you cared about me, Nora."

"A-all right. Go ahead, talk."

"Not here." His eyes shifted to Jack. "Privately."

"Go stuff yourself!" Jack yelled.

"Such a weak thing, a pulse." Adam slid a hand up Cuthbert's neck. "So easy to stop it forever."

"Wait!" Nora put her hands out. "I'll do whatever you want, but leave him alone!"

"Nora, no!" Jack grabbed her arm.

Adam smiled. "Come to the garden in half an hour. Don't climb the wall, come in by the prison door. Got that?"

"Yes! All right! Now, get away from Dr. Cuth!"

"Nora—"

"Jack, I have no choice."

"Promise," Adam purred.

"Yes! I promise!"

He held her eyes. "And don't forget. Your promise is the only thing that's keeping him alive."

He was gone.

Cuthbert stirred as they reached him, opened his eyes and sat up, flexing his shoulders. Then his eyebrows went up as he saw their faces. "What's wrong?"

"Nothing, now, I guess," Jack said lamely. "We thought you were sick."

"Well, I've felt better." He rubbed his neck and winced. "Remind me never again to fall asleep in my chair!"

IN THE LOBBY Nora turned and faced Jack. "Will you do me a favour? Take care of this?" She held out the talisman.

"Sure." He took it and slipped it into his shorts pocket.

"Make sure he doesn't get hold of it!"

"No sweat. Now what?"

"Now you're off the hook. It was my promise. I have to keep it, not you."

"Oh, no. You're not going near that place alone, not with him there." Jack stepped between her and the front door.

"I have to go! Jack, don't give me a hard time, please!"

"Right. We're both going."

She started organizing an argument, but the set of his jaw said she'd be wasting her breath. Besides, she really didn't want to go alone. And Jack was the only gleam of sanity in her nightmare.

"Maybe," she said, "just maybe, between here and the garden, a miracle will happen and we'll come up with a plan."

But fifteen minutes later, when they ducked into the ruined prison under the broken door, they had no plan and not even the beginnings of one.

This time no half-heard voices called to her, nothing touched her, as she walked along the dark corridor behind Jack, who held the flashlight. There was no sense of echoing hollows all around. She felt

164

as if all the evil here had drained off into the place where Adam waited, leaving the prison a crumbling shell.

When they came to the steel door that led into the garden, Jack stopped and waved her back. "Let me get out there first, just in case he's got some surprise waiting for us."

She hesitated. "Well, okay, but be careful!"

He wrestled the heavy door open. Sunlight and sweet air flooded into the grimy corridor. "Looks okay so far," he said, and stepped through.

As Nora moved to follow, the rectangle of sunlight began to narrow. The moment she realized what was happening she lunged forward, but she was one moment too late. The door slammed in her face with a boom that sent echoes shuddering through the building.

She tugged at the handle. She beat on the door with her hands. Nothing happened. It wasn't locked, couldn't be: the lock was broken. But it wouldn't budge. A frantic thudding came from the other side, then tapered off.

"Nora," came a velvety voice out of the darkness.

She set her back against the door and searched the corridor in front of her. She saw nothing but after-images of the sunlit doorway floating purple against the blackness.

"Nora, empty your pockets."

When she hesitated, something cold touched her wrist. Without her willing it, her right hand went into her pocket and came out with a handful of crushed petals. Her fingers opened and let them fall.

A hand closed over hers. A solid hand, strong as Jack's or stronger, but so cold! When she tried to pull free, his grip tightened. "Come with me, Nora."

"Where?" They were already moving, step by step through the lightless corridors. Adam seemed to need no light. Nora kept her eyes wide open, straining to see. Purple blotches drifted across her sight.

"Does it matter? We're together, that's all that counts. You won't ever leave me, Nora, will you?"

He's thinking of Ursula.

"Oh, yes, Ursula." His voice was a snake sliding over ice.

They walked on. Indigo bars striped the blackness. Light was creeping into the corridor from the entrance area. And once outside...

"No, no." He laughed gently. "Remember your promise!"

"I promised to meet you. I've done that."

"You were thinking to bind me again, weren't you? I'm long past binding. I'm so much stronger now, with all this new life inside me."

They stepped into the entrance area and he pulled her to a halt. "Look at me, and you'll see."

Unwilling, she turned to look at him. Even in this dim grey light, he looked solid, alive. You'd swear he was flesh and blood. A tall boy with a face so beautiful it made you catch your breath. Her right hand rose, fingers curved to touch his cheek. His mouth slowly curled up into a smile as he watched her face.

Enchanting... except for his eyes. Her hand halted in mid-air. His russet eyes, with that lick of hellfire that came from deep inside.

She forced her hand back to her side. From somewhere she found courage. "You killed them both, didn't you?"

"I had to. She chose him instead of me." He made a careless face, as if what he'd done should make sense to anyone. "But I made a mistake, killing myself. I admit it. I thought by burying the talisman I'd keep her bound to me for all eternity. That we'd be together forever. You see, I really did love her, Nora. I did. But it went wrong. Instead I was bound to this place, and she escaped me — again. It was the last mistake I'll ever make."

She couldn't look away from his eyes. The lick of hellfire filled them. It crept into her mind and wrapped a reddish haze around her thoughts.

166

"Nora, walk with me."

Dazed, she let him lead her through the room and under the door, out into the sunlight. Then she found herself climbing down the cliff, still in a dreamlike haze. Gentle hands helped her over the steep parts. "Don't worry. I won't let you fall."

On the beach she stood looking out over Georgian Bay to the horizon. Her feet were cold. She looked down to find herself ankle-deep in water. She tried to step back, but Adam's arm was a bar of iron around her shoulders. Her struggle dragged one sneaker off.

"Go on, you can do it." He was all gentle encouragement. "I know, I've done it. This is what I faced, that day. There's nothing out there, you'll see: nothing but death."

"But I don't want to die!"

"Don't be frightened, Nora. You're thinking about the last time, aren't you? When you drowned alone. It'll be better this time: you won't be alone. I'll be with you every moment, I promise."

All the while he talked they were moving deeper into the water. Now it was up to her waist, the cold striking through her clothes. His voice was like honey, clogging her panicked brain, but desperate thoughts kept breaking through. *Why?*

"Because we both drowned, once. Only, you came alive again, and I stayed dead. That's not fair, is it? This time, I'll be the one to come out alive."

"I don't understand."

"It's very simple." His breath chilled her ear. "Your life is the last one I need — almost. Maybe one more, old Cuthbert or that annoying Jack, and then I'll be totally free."

The stones slid under her feet. She was floating, then swimming. Stroking strongly, the way she used to love doing, speeding through the water. On and on, tirelessly, at home in the water.

A twist of her head, a look back. The cliff and the silhouette of the ruined prison were very far away. Too far.

She gasped, choked, started to thrash. Shock wiped the lulling haze from her mind. Panic grabbed hold.

It was happening again. She was drowning — again.

Leaden cold wrapped her arms and legs and dragged her down. She clawed at the glimmering surface, but it lifted away above, higher and higher, and the light dimmed. Darkness exploded in her mind.

Her last despairing thought was a cry.

Chapter 29

A Wreath of Blue

WHEN THE STEEL DOOR slammed, Jack's first impulse was to hurl himself at it and batter it down. After pounding at it for half a minute he realized how hopeless that was. It would get him nothing but more bruises than he already had.

Over the wall, then. Quick! He turned and started through the long grass. Two quick steps, three, four. Two more, not so fast. One slow step. One... more. He stopped.

Jack stood in the middle of the prison yard and gazed around. It was hot, with the stone walls radiating the day's sunshine. The air moved lazily, the trees stood almost motionless. Bees blundered among the black-eyed Susans.

It was hard to believe anything bad had ever happened here. This was a garden now, not a prison yard. Whatever evil had been done was long buried and gone.

Jack folded down with a tired sigh into the sweet-scented grass. In a corner of his mind he was dimly aware of something he should be doing, something vital. Too bad he couldn't recall what it was.

"So sleepy..." It would be wonderful just to close his eyes and rest, here in this golden pocket of peace. He rolled down flat on his back. Sleep rose around him like a tide of warm, dark water. Someone was calling his name, but the voice was distant, too far away to bother about, and not one he knew. He floated, deliciously limp, completely at peace. Peace....

"Ow!" Something sharp stung his fingers. A nose-scouring odour tore sleep into tatters. He sat up and looked at his thumb. It was bleeding. A thin, hard, wiry stem had thrust up under his hand: that must have done it. One of those blue-flowered vines that were all over the place. Most of its blossoms were crushed.

Vaguely and stupidly, he wondered at that. Then other questions slouched back into his mind. Why was he so stupid? Why had he been asleep?

A yellow gleam in the grass caught his eye. The snake ring. It must have fallen out of his pocket. He reached out to take it and then drew his hand back.

Something was happening. Vines were overgrowing the ring, trying to bury it, the way they'd tried to bury Nora... weird things....

No, wait. They weren't burying it. He got down on his hands and knees to get a closer look. His lips shaped a silent whistle. The vines were growing like mad, twining around the ring, forcing their thin stems in among the twists of gold, wrapping them around and around. When the vines stopped moving, the talisman had become a tiny blue wreath, with only flecks of gold glinting from among the petals.

Truly weird. Nora was right about those plants after all.

"Nora!"

He lurched to his feet in panic. She was gone, Adam had her, God only knew what they—

Then it hit him: he'd been under some kind of compulsion, and he'd been rescued. He'd been given a second chance. The flowers had done that for him. No, for Nora.

If there was still time! He scooped up the talisman (unexpectedly not anchored to the earth) and went to thrust it into his pocket, then decided not to. From now on, he would trust only his own hands. He kept the thing tight in his left fist, threw the climbing branch into position against the wall and swarmed up it. Dropped to the ground on the other side.

Now where? Where would Adam have taken her?

Forcing his whirling thoughts into ragged order, he made for the cliff top. At least there he'd find a view to the north. Halted there, breathing hard, he raked the beach with his eyes. Nobody there. Just rocks and waves and....

What was that? Something white, right at the water-line. He slithered down, snagged his heel on a rough place and rolled the last few yards, left hand still fisted. Bounced up, scrambled across to where the white thing bobbed in a few inches of water.

A sneaker. He picked it up. About Nora's size. On the inside of the heel someone, Nora or more likely her mother, had neatly penned NB with indelible ink.

He gazed out over the empty blue of Georgian Bay, and a blackness came down on his mind. He sat down on the stones and buried his head in his hands. The flower-wreathed talisman was still clutched in his left fist, almost forgotten.

Jack!

His head went up. So faint, so far, he wasn't even sure he'd heard it. He jumped up, he stared in every direction over the water. Still nothing.

He put his head back and howled. "Nora!"

Listened, eyes tight closed, breath stopped. Into the darkness of his mind Nora's cry came again. Fainter, weaker, but this time he could point to a direction. North and a little west.

She was out there, and she was alive, and her mind was her own. Kicking off his shoes, he floundered into the water, hurled a prayer at the heavens, and struck out toward the horizon.

NOT AGAIN. I won't drown again! Twisting in the chaos of water, where there was no up or down, Nora glimpsed a cloudy blue light in one direction. That had to be the surface. She thrust herself toward it.

171

Strong arms wrapped around her. *Don't be afraid! I'm here. We're together.*

She pushed back, wrestled to get free, famished for air, crazy with desperation. *Let me go! I won't drown again! I won't die!*

Look at me, Nora. Look at me!

No! She already knew the power of his eyes.

Still struggling, she grew sharply aware of his arms, how hard and thin they felt as they pressed against hers. She looked down and saw them, stick-thin, ivory-pale, except where weeds and slime blotched them with green and brown.

She was a prisoner in a cage of bone.

Horror stilled her. She turned her head, slow, dreading. A white, dead face pressed close to hers. The empty eye sockets — no, not empty, a tiny red flame lit their bony curves — they smiled at her. A voice called, still velvety-sweet.

I promised you wouldn't be alone. I always keep my promises.

Nora's silent scream sent bubbles gushing from her straining lungs.

JACK TROD WATER, gasping. A terror not his own had just seared his mind. Near, now — but where?

Froth whitened the surface a few yards away.

He dove. He found Nora fighting a nightmare of weed and slime, a thing that must have lain rotting in the depths for twenty years. It turned his way, still circling her with one arm. The other reached for his face, bony fingers clawing at his eyes, jagged grin open wide.

The talisman burned like blue neon in Jack's left fist. As the horror lunged at him he thrust the snake ring, with its aureole of sky-blue flowers, between its grinning jaws. The teeth bit down on Jack's fingers. He let the talisman go.

Chapter 30

Free

"AT LEAST TWICE, I thought I wasn't going to make it."

Most of a day had passed since they swam to shore together. Jack lay flat in a bed of matted grass in the middle of the secret garden and gazed up at the pale morning sky.

Nora looked up from where she was poking along the prison wall, apparently picking flowers. "I would have towed you, if you'd started to sink. You'd still be alive."

"I know. That's what kept me going — the thought of being hauled home like a leaky dinghy, after I'd gone out to rescue you."

"But you did rescue me. If you hadn't found me, and used the talisman..." She shook her head, came over to sit down beside him, dumped whatever she'd been gathering to one side, and carefully picked up his bandaged left hand. (The doctor at the West Parry Sound Health Centre had told him he was lucky to still have all his fingers, and he'd better steer clear of old decrepit buildings after this. He promised he would.)

"If it it hadn't been for you," Nora went on, "I wouldn't be here now. I'd be out there." She tipped her head toward the lake.

"I can't take much credit. I might still be sleeping in the grass if something hadn't waked me up."

"Something. Or someone?"

"Who knows?" After a moment he asked, "No sign of Adam? No dreams?"

"Nothing. I slept like a baby for the first night in a week!" She glanced up at the prison wall. "I wonder, with him gone, will the others go too?"

"What others?"

For a moment he thought she wasn't going to answer. Then she looked at him unsmiling and said, "There were ghosts. In the jail." He opened his mouth but shut it when she held up her hand. "They were there. I won't argue about it."

"Who's arguing?" He twitched his bandaged hand feebly and she picked it up again. There, that was more like it.

Their parents had arrived that morning after breakfast. After a tense half-hour conference that included the two elder McKies, Nora's mother, Staff Sgt. Rose and both Dr. Loftuses, Beth had looked at Jack and Nora, nodded at the door, and made a pushing motion with her fingers.

They escaped at once, enormously relieved. Outside the school, Nora caught Jack's unmaimed right hand hand and started up the hill. "There's something I've got to check."

For the last ten minutes she had been searching in the corners of the garden, while Jack watched her and wished he could scrape together the courage to talk about things that really mattered. Like life, and death, and love, and.... Well, maybe later.

"I think we're off the hook with the police," he said. "Though I'll bet that cop will have his suspicions of me till his dying day. And none of our parents are happy with the answers they're getting either, you can see that."

"They're better off not knowing the whole truth," Nora said firmly. "Look at this." She scooped something from beside her and tipped a handful of debris onto his chest.

He sat up and grabbed at the pieces that fell from his T-shirt. "What's this junk?"

"That's all I could find of the blue-flowered vines. They were gone from around my window this morning, too. Didn't you notice?"

He held a withered stem that crumbled in his fingers. The scattering petals were more grey than blue.

"They're both really gone, now," Nora said. "Adam, and Ursula. It's over. Thank heaven!"

"Ursula?"

"Who else? Remember he said he'd wanted to bind her to him forever, but she escaped him? She didn't escape after all. She was here all the time, watching. Keeping an eye on him. Many eyes."

Nora lifted an ashen petal on her fingertip and let the breeze carry it away. "And now she's free."

About the author

PATRICIA BOW lives in Kitchener, Ontario. She has written several other books for young people. To find out more about Patricia and her work, visit www.execulink.com/~thebows/patricia.htm.